WHAT DO PEOPLE SAY ABOUT MIKE HERR'S BOOKS ?

(The Bones of the Kuhina Nui) is a GREAT mystery story . . . but more importantly it is culturally correct. Many stories written about Hawaii . . . make our legends and stories seem trite tho they are very important to our culture and beliefs.

Gail Gomes, Waianae, Amazon.com.

(The Old Queen's Treasure) is the third in Herr's "Kohala Coast Thriller" series centering on the (Pono family). He's crafted an engrossing yarn, much of it rooted in the interwoven cultural tidbits about ancient burial practices, traditional reverence for the iwi (bones), antiquities, even the Hawaiian martial art of lua.

Betty Shimabukuro, Star Bulletin.

(The Old Queen's Treasure) contains just enough intrigue to keep the reader interested . . . the attention to details for things Hawaiian is so good that you can almost smell the plumeria.

Cathy Tallyn, Rossmoor News.

A NEW kind of Hawaiian fiction is emerging. Like its writers, it is neither wholly of the islands, nor of the mainland. It is both. This new genre of "hapa-fiction" -- male, ironic, hard-boiled in a Raymond Chandler kind of way -- is well represented in the work of . . . Michael A. Herr . . . those who live here will be enchanted, amused and charmed . . . The settings, too, are full of rich local detail.

Michael Egan, *Is 'Chicken Skin' a Local Delicacy*, Star Bulletin.

Mr. Herr manages to tell several stories within one, using a finely tuned sense of humor and a knowledge of the islands to keep his readers fully engaged.

Diane in Davis, Amazon.com.

I grew up on Oahu . . . have lived in SoCal for 40 years and reading your wonderful books is like going back home! I look forward to your next book.

Charlotte Patterson, Costa Mesa, CA

There is much Hawaiian history in The Old Queen's Treasure.

Pat Elliott, BookLoons Reviews.

Herr spins a tale of history, mystery, family dysfunction and the value of family ties in an exotic setting.

Shirley Wetzel for OVER MY DEAD BODY, The Mystery Magazine Online.

A natural storyteller (Mr. Herr's) tales are full of life, well-researched island details and obvious respect for (Hawaii). Each Kohala Coast thriller is better than the last.

Catherine Tarleton, author "Potluck: Stories That Taste Like Hawaii".

If you've ever been to Hawaii or are planning to visit, this is a "must read!" Even if you know nothing about Hawaii, it's still a great mystery with a charming family at the center . . . Mr. Herr's writing is wonderfully descriptive, accurate in its detail and humorous in just the right amount. The plots are involved and keep you interested.

Cynthia A. Geesey (Amazon Kindle Review)

As a lover of anything that has to do with the big island of Hawaii, I wasn't able to put this book down! Right from the very first page of the book, ancient Hawaiian culture is weaved into the story . . . Although the mystery is captivating, the author's knowledge of both ancient Hawaii and modern day big Island are what truly sets this book apart from most other Hawaii-based fiction. I highly recommend this book to all, local or those . . . that wish they were.

Taryn (Amazon Kindle Review)

. . . these books are mysterious with old lore and traditions. But yet, Teri is in the current world . . . dealing with her family, especially her mother. A good thriller to curl up with.

Hayley K., *Hanging off the Wire* (Blogspot)

. . . the three criminals who inhabit ("The Old Queen and the Maui Maiden") are among the most memorable you'll ever encounter in the genre. Herr has joined my very short list of favorite crime writers.

Doug Hergert (The Rossmoor News)

DEDICATION

To Stan, who kept pushing until we took the cruise to Hawaii from San Francisco.

No entertainment is so cheap as reading nor any pleasure so lasting.

DISCLAIMER

This is a work of fiction. The characters are figments of my imagination. They don't exist! Any resemblance, except for actual historical figures who may be used fictionally, is purely coincidental. Locations and physical features of the island of Hawai`i may have been altered to fit the needs of my story.

಄಄಄

First Printing,

ISBN 978-0-578-19459-2

Published by Michael A Herr

Printing by Mira Digital Publishing

Printed in the United States of America

The Old Queen's Deadly Cruise

A Kohala Coast Mystery

by

Michael A. Herr

1

Saturday, September 8, 11:57 p.m.

Over on the Big Island, in Kona, a female police dispatcher working the night shift had some unexpected excitement to deal with.

"All units, report of a man with a gun at Hulihee Palace. Very large man, dark complexion. Proceed with caution."

Just over a minute later the dispatcher had more urgent news to broadcast.

"All units, officer down. Code 3. Officer down, Hulihee Palace. Ambulance and paramedic units responding. All units, officer down. *Officer down!*"

2

Along the Queen Ka'ahumanu Highway, heading south.

Detective Sergeant Edward Kakuhaupio Akamai, Big Ed to his friends and other veteran officers, got the message just as he was driving through Kona on the Queen Ka'ahumanu Highway. Detective Sergeant Akamai was tired. He had just come off a six-hour shift. A personal duty shift far up the coast and close to the ocean. It was a shift he shared with a number of other Hawaiian men, some of them police some of them not. It had been a matter of surveillance, not unlike a police stakeout, but this surveillance had been going on for decades and would continue for many more. It had resulted in death more than once, but never on Detective Sergeant Akamai's watch. Big Ed was tired and wanted nothing more than to get to his tiny one-bedroom one-bathroom apartment down by Keauhou. The apartment was all he had since his wife of thirty-two years had claimed, with her lawyer's help, their house for herself and herself alone.

Big Ed flipped a switch on his dashboard turning on the flashing blue headlights of his unmarked Ford Crown Victoria. He pulled a blue bubble light free from the dash with his right hand, passed it to his left hand, reached out the open window and placed it onto the roof of his car. The strong magnet in the base held it in place as he flipped its 'on' switch.

Fortunately, he was just at the turnoff for Palani Road when the message came in. With lights on but no siren Big Ed whipped down Palani, past the Kona Coast Shopping Center; even this late still illuminated by its parking lot lights. He briefly crossed the center line as Palani Road became Ali'i Drive. Once on Ali'i he turned off his blue lights and his headlights. He turned off the bubble light, pulled it back in and dropped it onto the floor beside him.

Big Ed pulled over to the curb just past the entrance to Hulihee Palace. For a big man, Big Ed moved quickly and smoothly. He rolled out of the driver's side door just as a large black shadow vaulted over the lava rock wall of the Palace. The shadow crouched on the sidewalk, bunching up its muscles prior to springing into action.

"Francisco, relax. You might be bigger than me, but I'm faster an' I know more dirty tricks than you . . . even with your lua training."

Francisco Na'ale recognized the truth of the Detective Sergeant's words, blew out the breath he had been holding and, relaxing his muscles, stood up and allowed the Detective Sergeant to grip his elbow and guide him back down the sidewalk and through the open gates to the Palace.

"You, Big Ed? Whachoo doing up so late?"

"Same question back at you, Francisco," Big Ed said. In the distance Big Ed heard the sirens of other police cars targeting on the Palace.

Stepping in through the gate, Big Ed saw a police officer lying on the lawn while a broken sprinkler head behind him poured a gusher of water onto his back. For a minute Big Ed's gut clenched. Then the officer levered himself up off the lawn, swore quite energetically, and moved out from under the torrent of water pouring down on him.

"You okay?" Big Ed called to the officer even as he and the large Hawaiian man squished across the lawn.

"Yeah, yeah, I'm okay."

Big Ed took his portable radio off his belt, thumbed it's call switch and spoke.

"Maggie, this is Detective Sergeant Akamai. Call off the other units. I'm on scene at Hulihee and everything is under control. No officer needs assistance. No one injured."

The dispatcher in her cubicle listened to the communication as it came in, toggled her switch and sent the following:

"All units, Code 4. Slow it down boys. Everything's under control. Hulihee Palace secure. Big Ed is there," and to ensure that everyone slowed down and went back to their regular patrols, "officer is uninjured, repeat, uninjured. Over an' out."

The three patrol cars racing to the scene turned off their lights and sirens, and yet they still managed to creep past the palace slowly enough so that they could observe everything going on.

Clicking his microphone one officer said, "Hoo, looks like Parker gonna have a lot of writing to do tonight."

Another officer spoke into his radio adding, "Yeah, an' maybe he gonna have to do it standing up after Big Ed kick his tail aroun' the block."

Big Ed turned and looked over at the street and the patrol cars sliding by. Under his gaze the three officers picked up speed and headed back out on patrol.

Big Ed turned back to the thoroughly soggy officer standing in front of him.

₧₨

"You okay, Parker?" Big Ed asked again.

"What the frick do you think?" Officer Parker answered, his silver shield glinting in the moonlight. Officer Parker, a haole who had joined the force on the Big Island only four months ago, stood on the front lawn of Hulihee Palace, just to the left of the entrance. Water ran off him in streams. When he shifted his feet, his shoes squished. A skid path showed where he had tripped over a sprinkler head as the sprinklers came on for their nightly duty. The broken black plastic sprinkler head lay on the lawn, a few feet in front of the gushing water . . . the same water that had poured down onto Officer Parker, thoroughly drenching him.

Officer Parker looked up and stood a little straighter when he recognized the Detective Sergeant, with the shiny gold badge, standing in front of him.

Big Ed looked over Officer Parker's shoulder at the front entrance to the Hulihee Palace. Draped across the entryway, from one pillar to the opposite pillar, hung a banner made from three king-size sheets *("Property of Queen's Beach Resort Hotel"* printed on one corner in small letters) stitched together and held up by a length of nylon rope. In giant red letters across the banner ran the words

Malama Pono O Ka `Āina
Imua Lanakila

Detective Sergeant Edward Kakuhaupio Akamai, translated to himself . . . *"Making Things Right with the Land - - - Forward to Victory".* Noble sentiments, but this was not the way, at least not in his view.

The Sergeant noted the 9mm handgun in Officer Parker's right hand. It too glistened with drops of water still.

"You fired your weapon, Officer?"

"Uhhh, it discharged accidentally Sergeant, when I tripped and fell."

"Uh-huh, and you had it out because . . ."

"Well, the call I got said there was someone vandalizing the Palace," Officer Parker spoke with more assurance now, "and when I got here I saw this guy running away. I called to him to stop but he wouldn't."

"So you pulled your weapon. Were you going to shoot a man who was running away, who had not threatened you?"

"Oh, no Sergeant, I was just preparing myself for any eventuality. At most I would have fired a warning shot."

The Sergeant's face froze.

"WE DON'T DO WARNING SHOTS, OFFICER."

Officer Parker seemed to shrink a little more into the sodden lawn.

"No, Sergeant . . . I meant to say . . ."

"Quiet. Don't dig that hole you're in right now any deeper."

Big Ed looked Officer Parker up and down. Inwardly he marveled that Parker had been hired. Experienced, yes, but not with the multiple cultures found here on the Big Island. City boy. No experience with the aina of Hawaii.

Big Ed sighed and thought, *At least no one died tonight.*

"Okay Parker. Take down that banner and bring it to the station with you. Get some dry clothes on and write your report. Leave it for the Lieutenant. He'll want something to amuse him when he gets in this morning."

Big Ed turned to Francisco.

"Now you, Francisco. You come with me. We're gonna take a little drive."

"Sergeant, do you want to borrow my handcuffs?" Officer Parker asked.

Big Ed shook his head as he looked back at the drenched officer.

"No, won't be necessary . . . will it, Francisco?"

"No, Big Ed, no need."

Big Ed walked with Francisco back to his idling Crown Vic, went around to the driver's side. Francisco started to open the rear passenger side door, but Big Ed said, "No, get in the front". Francisco moved to the front passenger door and got into the car, his size 12 feet squishing water onto the floor..

Big Ed stood beside the open driver side door. He took his cellphone out of his pocket and dialed a number. Francisco couldn't make out what Big Ed said, but he did hear Big Ed's last words, "Mahalo, I owe you one."

Big Ed put away his cellphone, pulled the blue buld light from the roof and slid in behind the wheel. He placed the blue light onto the dash and looked over at Francisco.

"You wet too?"

"No, Big Ed, only my feet. When da haole police fall down . . . da bullet miss me by a mile."

"That's good. Otherwise I'd have been stuck here for hours and writing reports for even more. Might even have had to call the coroner. Buckle up."

Big Ed put his car in gear and pulled away, heading back up to the Queen Ka'ahumanu Highway. He turned east toward Hilo.

Francisco knew the way, and knew that just on the outskirts of Hilo was the Hawaii County Correctional Center, H-Triple-C, as the locals called it. Francisco wondered how long he might have to spend there.

3

The two men sat in silence as they drove through the night. The car climbed up the Mamalahoa Highway, known mostly as the Belt road, until it reached the outskirts of Volcano Village. Off to their right the two men saw a bright glow bouncing off the undersides of the clouds above.

"The Lady still awake," Francisco said.

"Yep, she don't sleep much lately . . . and neither do cops."

The car began the long drive downhill to Hilo.

"Francisco Na'ale," Big Ed said. He let the name wander around through the car while he thought.

"Francisco you still work baggage at Kona International, don't you?"

"Yeah."

"So, if they find out you got arrested, would they fire you?"

"Mos' probably," Francisco answered. He stared out the window into the night for a while.

"No can have a criminal record an' work the airport."

Big Ed nodded to himself and drummed his thumbs on the steering wheel.

"So . . . why take the chance . . . just to hang a banner?"

"Because . . . because we got to do something to take our land back. We got to keep working to bring back the Hawaiian nation," Francisco swiveled around in his seat to face Big Ed. "You should know that, you're Hawaiian."

A grin spread across Big Ed's face revealing his perfectly white teeth.

"Yep, one hundred percent."

"See, see what I mean. You're kanaka maoli an' you should be working with us to restore our nation."

"Francisco, there's all sorts of ways people work toward restoring the Hawaiian nation. Some of them aren't going to work. Some of them may."

Francisco slumped in his seat.

"Now you sounding jus' like Koakane. You know him, right?"

"Oh, we've met a few times," Big Ed glanced over at Francisco, "He wouldn't have approved what you did tonight."

"An' that's why me an' some others no more with him."

The two men drove some more in silence. Each sunk in his own thoughts.

Francisco sat up a little straighter as they approached the buildings that comprised H Triple-C. To his surprise they drove past the compound and on down into Hilo.

Big Ed turned left onto Mamalahoa Highway, drove through Kea'au and finally turned left onto Hulani. After driving two blocks Big Ed turned right onto Hinano Street. He drove a little way up the street and pulled right into an empty parking lot.

Francisco's eyes opened wide when he saw where they were. Not H Triple-C . . . Don's Grill. A local restaurant, and a very popular one. But not at almost four o'clock in the morning. Light shone through windows toward the rear of the restaurant.

Big Ed got out of his car, waved to Francisco to follow him and walked around the restaurant. The two men got to the back door to the kitchen. Big Ed pulled the door open, motioned to Francisco that he should enter and then followed him inside.

There was only one other person in the kitchen, a cook with a potbelly that needed both his tee shirt and an apron to cover it.

"Hey, Henry, my usual table?" Big Ed called cheerily.

The cook spat in the sink.

"Wake me up fo' dis? You pushin' it Big Ed."

"Good morning to you too," Big Ed said. He stepped over to an enormous coffee pot, put his hand on the outside of the pot, nodded in satisfaction and proceeded to draw himself a mug of midnight black coffee. He took a sip.

"Oh, yeah, that'll get you going." He drew another mug of coffee from the pot, handed it to Francisco and moved out through the swinging doors into the dark restaurant. The cook swiveled his head to look Francisco up and down.

Once through the door, Big Ed paused to flick a light switch beside the door, brightening the near half of the restaurant. He walked over to a table for two, stopping only to gather two sets of cutlery wrapped in napkins. Big Ed placed the cutlery on the table, set down his mug, pulled out a chair and sat. He looked up at Francisco who stood beside the table his mug in his hand.

"So, you need someone to pull out your chair for you?"

Francisco sat down.

The two men sat in silence blowing on their hot coffee each time before taking a sip.

Francisco hadn't been to Don's Grill for several years so he looked around at the restaurant. Tables mostly with just a few booths along one wall. Posters, pictures and some memorabilia hung on the walls. He smiled when he saw a medium-sized Hawaiian flag hanging between a picture of King Kamehameha and another of Queen Ka'ahumanu. When he looked away he saw Big Ed staring at him. Big Ed nodded, but didn't say anything.

Francisco started to open his mouth, a question forming in his mind, but just then the cook came through the swinging doors pushing a cart. He pushed the cart over to the table where Big Ed and Francisco sat and proceeded to unload it. Soon Big Ed and Francisco were each facing a plate of loco moco, a double helping on each plate, a smaller plate of buttered toast, a small bowl each of sliced papaya and smaller bowls of guava jam. There was also a white carafe of coffee in the center of the table so they could refill as needed.

The cook turned and began to push the cart back toward the kitchen.

"Hey, Henry. Mahalo plenty, brah," Big Ed called.

The cook waved one hand in the air and, not deigning to turn around, called back, "A'ole pilikia . . . but no wake me up so early again, eh?" And with that he pushed the cart into the kitchen, leaving the two doors flapping back and forth for a minute.

ℬↃↁ

Big Ed mopped up the remaining gravy with his last bit of toast. He took a sip of coffee, his third cup, and leaned back in his chair.

"So, Francisco, you want to restore the old Hawaii."

"Yeahhhh."

"Which means you want to protect the old Hawaii, right?"

"R-right."

"And you're willing to give of yourself to restore old Hawaii, and protect old Hawaii? Our ways? Our culture? Our heritage?"

Francisco leaned forward over the table, his forearms pressing down on its surface.

"Das right. I would give myself, my life to see our aina restored, our culture brought back."

"Hmmm," Big Ed said softly. "Then I have an offer for you. One that I hope you can't refuse. One that I think will match your desires. One that you will never, never ever tell anyone about."

ℬↃↁ

Back out in the parking lot, Big Ed got into his car, a toothpick hanging from the side of his mouth. Francisco stood alongside Big Ed's car as the early morning sun began to lighten the day.

"Okay, Francisco. No more stupid stuff. You think about all I said, and when you're sure you've got an answer, call me."

"Sure thing, Big Ed. I could tell you now . . ."

"No, I want you to really think about this. After all, it's not something you can go back on. You wouldn't break away from this like you did from Koakane's group."

Big Ed used the toothpick on his teeth, inspected the result and looked back again at Francisco.

"By the way, where is Koakane these days?"

"Oh, I think maybe he wen' off wit' his girlfriend an' her mother an' her seestahs. Maybe take vacation."

Big Ed nodded then he turned the key and started his car.

Francisco looked around at the empty parking lot.

"How I'm s'posed to get home?"

"Like they say on that game show, Francisco, 'Phone a friend, phone a friend,'" said Big Ed before pulling out of the parking lot and heading back toward Kailua-Kona.

Francisco stood there watching Big Ed's taillights fade into the distance. He patted his pockets, found his phone, took it out and turned it back on.

Muttering to himself he scrolled through his contacts.

"Who's gonna be willing to come pick me up this early? Maybe him?"

Standing there, Francisco listened as his first call went to voicemail.

4
The Pono Family Hale

Four coffee mugs, the coffee in them cooling fast, sat around the kitchen of the Pono Family Hale. Papers were spread out on the Formica top of the kitchen table. Outside the kitchen and down the hallway frantic scramblings could be heard. Urgent voices called out.

"Teri, have you seen my sunglasses?"

"Look on top of your head."

"Ha-ha, funny . . . oops, there they are."

"Mom . . . hey, Mom, do you think I should take these slacks?"

"Sure, if you think you can still get in them."

A noise as if a giant bunny was hopping around on the wood flooring ensued.

"Yeah, still can. Just got to squeeze a little."

"Shari, how much money should I take?"

"Only a little more than you can afford to lose."

"But I can't afford to lose any."

"You gonna have a pretty dull time."

₧₧

A herd of stampeding deer rushed into the kitchen, only to separate out into the three remaining daughters of the Pono family; Teri, Lori and Shari. Their mother, Haunani, followed them in at a more sedate pace. Shari claimed the kitchen table as the spot for her to deposit her suitcase. She spread it open and continued tucking items into the corners of the suitcase and taking items out to refold and pack again -- blouses and skirts and underwear and miscellaneous items.

Teri and Lori dropped their suitcases on the floor and began to imitate Shari's method of organization.

Haunani set her closed and locked suitcase on the floor by the kitchen door. She even had a luggage strap wrapped around it and a tag with her name and address attached to the handle. Her suitcase was so old that it didn't even have wheels.

Haunani responded to a knock at the kitchen door by opening the door and planting a kiss on the cheek of the handsome Hawaiian man who stood there. She gently dragged him in by his elbow.

"Koakane, thank goodness, maybe you can bring some order to this place."

Koakane smiled, his perfectly white teeth seemed to brighten the room. Teri noticed that he had done his shoulder-length hair into a ponytail today. She wished that her hair could look as good as his midnight-black hair. She wished her sisters and mother weren't here so that she could run her fingers through his hair. She also wished that her hair looked half as good as her sisters. There was Lori with her short cut, two swoops with a brush and she was good to go. Shari had her hair styled, as usual, but in the version of some rock star probably since Teri didn't recognize it. And Haunani. Haunani's hair had started to change color a year ago, and by now it was pure shining white. Whiter than the snow on top of Mauna Kea. Teri ran her fingers through her own hair and cringed when she realized she had forgotten, again, to wash it. She began to imagine small creatures taking up residence in her hair. Teri looked up to see Koakane smiling at her . . . or maybe just grinning at the pile of lacy underwear she held in her hands.

Teri stuffed the underwear in her hands underneath a stack of blouses in her suitcase, rose and stepped over to Koakane. She gave him a small kiss on the cheek.

"Our savior," she said.

"Our luggage carrier," Lori said.

"Our sister's main squeeze," Shari said.

"Main?" said Koakane. "You mean she got others," he added with a jealous look at Teri.

Teri slapped Koakane on the shoulder, "Be serious," she said. And to her two sisters she said, "Come on, finish packing, we have to get going if we want to catch our flight."

"Yeah," Koakane said, "traffic bad out on the highway. I think maybe something happened this morning down in Kailua-Kona."

∞∞

The three girls finished packing their suitcases and Koakane got busy loading them all into the back of his pickup truck. He checked each suitcase to be sure it was secure and wound up typing piece of rope around Shari's suitcase in order to hold it together.

∞∞

Back inside the house all four women finished loading carry-on bags with essentials for the flight. Books, magazines, eye shades, ear plugs, chewing gum, snacks. When Teri saw Haunani putting a water bottle in her bag she quickly took it away and emptied it.

"What?" Haunani said.

"Mom, no more liquids through the gate. Take the empty bottle and fill it up once we're inside."

Haunani made a sound of disgust but zipped up her carry-on.

"Got your driver's license?"

"No," Haunani said, and before Teri could say anything else, Haunani added, "But I got my Hawaiian i.d. card since you girls made me give up my driver's license."

"Well, that's what I meant, Mom. An' you know it was . . ."

"I know, I know. Only for my own good an' because I had problems for a while there. But I'm okay now."

"Still better you don't drive," Shari said from a safe distance across the room.

Shari glanced out the window at Koakane loading his pickup.

"Soooo, Teri. Whose room you gonna stay in at the hotel?"

"I'm staying with Mom, her room,"

"Ohhh, not maybe in Koakane's room?"

Teri got busy looking for her coffee cup.

Lori, for once, chimed in on Shari's side.

"Say, Teri, how many dates have you and Koakane gone on now? Two?"

"I think maybe next time will be their third date," Shari said.

"Third?"

"Yeah, third." Shari said. "An' you know what they say about the third date . . . it's put out or forget it time."

Getting bold now, Lori asked, "Have you two done it yet?"

Before Teri could respond to her sisters Haunani spoke up, "You two, leave your sister alone."

Teri let out a sigh.

Haunani opened the kitchen door and looked outside.

"Anyhow, if Teri doesn't want him . . . I'll take him," Haunani said back over her shoulder as she headed toward her car, a Toyota Highlander V6 . . . the one she no longer drove.

All three girls stood in the doorway, their mouths open in wonder.

"Well, come on," Haunani waved, "let's go to Vegas."

℘ↄ℆

Haunani walked over and got into the front passenger seat while Lori climbed into the back. Both shut their doors and rolled down their windows. Koakane was already in the driver's seat of his small pickup as, without any hesitation, Teri walked around and opened the passenger side door. She looked over at the Toyota and saw Shari standing by the open driver's side door. Shari smiled at Teri and then pursed her lips as she made kissing noises. Teri stuck her tongue out at Shari and Shari replied with a rude hand gesture. Both women entered their respective vehicles, doors closed, engines started and the pickup pulled out followed closely by the Toyota.

At the bottom of the road that led up to the Pono Family Hale, both cars turned left onto the highway that led to Kona International Airport.

Teri could just barely hear Shari singing "Viva Las Vegas" from the Toyota behind them.

5

Kona International Airport

Koakane pulled up and parked his pickup in the loading zone at the Kona International Airport. Shari pulled up behind him with the Toyota. Teri got out of the pickup while Shari, Lori and Haunani unfolded themselves from the Toyota. A tall good-looking porter with a Hawaiian Airlines shirt and ball cap pushing a luggage cart rolled up and began loading the group's suitcases onto his cart.

"Aloha, Jesse, where's Francisco?"

After looking behind him to make sure Francisco wasn't sneaking up on him Jesse said, "Da lazy buggah. He call me an' say he got other stuff to do, an' can I fill in fo' him."

"Hmmm," Koakane said, "too bad, I was hoping maybe I could say hello to him."

Standing beside Koakane, Teri put her hand on his shoulder.

"You haven't seen him since he and the others split off from your group, have you?"

Koakane shook his head.

"Okay, I'll park the truck and be right back. Shari! Leave that poor boy alone and let's park the car and truck."

Shari wrinkled her nose at Koakane, but she also let go of Jesse's arm. She brushed her hip up against Jesse as she turned back to the Toyota. Jesse followed her with his eyes as she walked to the car and got in on the driver's side. She blew Jesse a kiss.

Koakane and Shari pulled away and headed for the long-term parking lot.

As Jesse followed the cars with his eyes, Haunani stepped up behind him and rapped her knuckles on the top of his head.

"C'mon you kanaka, we got a plane to catch," she said.

"Yes, auntie," Jesse replied as he wheeled the luggage cart toward baggage check-in. He rubbed the top of his head with one hand and steered the cart with his other.

₧₧

Koakane and Shari boarded the shuttle that would take them from the parking lot back to the terminal.

"So, how's it going with you and my sister?"

Koakane gave a slightly lopsided smile.

"Going okay . . . I guess."

"You guess?"

Koakane just shrugged.

Shari saw she wasn't going to get any more out of him, so the two of them sat in silence all the way back to the terminal.

₧₧

After checking in and getting through TSA, the five of them went into the little café at the side of the square, found a table and had small servings of ice cream while waiting for their flight to be called.

6

Kailua Kona

His hair still wet from the shower that had removed the sweat . . . the sweat of nearly getting shot, the sweat of thinking he was going to jail . . . Francisco moved quickly along the sidewalk, dodging early morning tourists mixed in with other locals like himself. Everyone with someplace to go.

He crossed Hualalai Road, stopping halfway across in order to avoid being run over by a tourist who was taking in all the sights and little of the traffic.

"Hey, haole, try wait next time," Francisco shouted after the tourist. Then he gave a rueful grin as he noticed that the 'haole' tourist was actually Japanese.

Once safely across the street Francisco joined the other members of his group at the Kona Koffee Kafe on the corner of the block. Despite the cutesy name, the coffee served there was good . . . and they had donuts. Francisco's group had commandeered the only table outside the Kafe. A large dinner plate stacked with donuts sat in the center of the round plastic table. Frank Palani reached across the table and handed Francisco a cup of black coffee, steam still curling from its surface.

"Mahalo, Frank," Francisco said as he took a sip of the blessed hot liquid.

"No problem, Francisco. An' five dollar you owe."

"Five dollars for one cup?"

"An' your share of da donuts."

"Oh . . . yeah, sorry my brain still not working."

"How come you so late?" Greyson asked. "You know I can't take too long, I got a group going out with me for a sea kayak tour." Greyson worked for Kona Sea Tours as a guide.

"Where you go?" asked Vincent, he was not as pressed for time as the surfboard shop where he worked was only two blocks further down the road and didn't open for another hour.

"Keauhau Bay," Greyson answered.

"Should be good today," Vincent said.

Francisco rummaged in his pocket, brought out a money clip with the Hawaiian flag on it, counted out five dollars and slapped them down in front of Palani.

Palani picked up the bills one at a time, slowly folded the bills and put them into his shirt pocket. He tapped the pocket to verify that the money had arrived there safely.

"Sooo?" said Greyson, "How come you late?"

Francisco took another sip of his coffee and half a chocolate covered donut before answering.

"The police picked me up."

All of the other three reacted strongly. Vincent choked on his coffee. Palani rocked back in his chair and nearly fell over. Greyson set his cup down on the table so roughly that some of it sloshed out. He grabbed a napkin from the pile on the donut platter and mopped up the spill.

Francisco went ahead and related the events of the previous evening, leaving out only the part when Big Ed made him a curious offer.

"Eh, Big Ed not so bad," Palani said. "Bye um bye he stop in and order lunch when I'm working. I give him extra fries. My boss try tell him no need pay, but Big Ed always leave da money . . . an' a big tip."

"Shoots, dat greasy spoon you work at . . . best tip you can get about that place is . . . Don't Eat There," Vincent said.

Palani broke off a piece of cake donut and threw it at Vincent. Vincent threw it back. Palani broke off a bigger piece.

"Cut it out," Francisco said in a voice that meant business.

"We need to talk about what more we can do to push our sovereignty movement forward," he added.

The four men sat silent for a minute, drinking coffee and eating more donuts. Palani ate the piece of cake donut that he had intended to throw at Vincent.

Greyson drank some coffee and cleared his throat before speaking.

"You know, the kahu at my church talked about something this weekend. Something that maybe we should think about," he paused and swallowed more of his coffee.

"So? What did the priest say?" asked Vincent.

"Well," Greyson replied, "he talked about the aina, about how the land has changed. He said that some people say the aina is sick, but the way he figures it's not sick. It's weak. And he said that's why there's so much trouble . . . so much homelessness . . . so much bad things happening."

"'Cuz of the land?" Francisco asked.

"Yeah," Greyson answered, "because of the land. We, the Hawaiian people, are tied to the land naturally. We're one with the land. And if the land is weak, then so are we. If we want to get stronger, get healthier, then we need to strengthen the land. Us . . . and the aina, we're one."

The men sat and thought.

"You know," Vincent said, "the governor," all four of the men paused to spit on the ground, "said the other day that he is considering approving Traditional Hawaiian Burial Practices . . ."

"Sheet, why da hell he got to 'approve' dat? Is our culture. Is our heritage. Is our way of life! We no need his 'approval'. Hell, I nevah vote for da buggah anyways," and having made his point Francisco took another donut.

Heads nodded in agreement as one of the men said "Me too" and another said "Shoot, he's not even Hawaiian . . . he's Korean."

"Let's go back," Greyson said. "If we all agree that the aina is weak . . . how do we make it strong again?"

"You know," said Vincent, "I wen' over Honolulu a couple weeks ago. Visit my sister an' her family. Turned out she had to work one day, an' my nephew had a field trip from his school. So I wen' with him. We went to the Bishop Museum. You been there?"

Greyson nodded yes, Palani and Francisco shook their heads.

"Well," Vincent continued, "one thing stuck in my mind. I never see so many lei niho palaoa in one place. They must have hundreds hanging behind glass on display there."

"So?" said Palani.

"So . . . each of those lei niho used to belong to a chief or chiefess, an Ali'i from the old days. An' you know, those lei niho were important. They held the mana of the Ali'i. An' they used to be buried with the chiefs when they died. They took their bones, wrapped 'em in kapa and buried them . . . with their lei niho way away in some hidden cave, or deep in a lava tube. That way the mana from the chiefs stayed with the land."

Vincent paused and leaned back in his chair cradling his coffee mug in his hands.

Palani broke the silence.

"Sooo . . . what are you saying?"

Vincent leaned back in toward the table.

"I think maybe if we took all those lei niho from the museum, and if we reburied them up in the mountains on each island, then maybe that would help our aina get strong again. And if our aina got strong again, then our people would get strong again."

The group was silent.

Greyson put his coffee mug down on the table and stood up.

"I say we do it. We return the lei niho of our ancient Ali'i to the land, to the aina where they belong. Even if we can't reunite the lei niho with the bones of the Ali'i, we can reunite them with the land," he remained standing.

Palani stood. Vincent stood. And finally Francisco stood. They all reached across the table and joined hands.

All four sat back down.

"When do we do this?" Palani asked.

"Well, I think first we need to check out the museum. Figure out how to get in . . . and figure out how to get out again. I can take a day off next week and fly over."

"I can go with you, my boss owes me a day off," said Vincent.

"I'll go with you," Greyson said, "I'd like to see the museum again."

Francisco took another mouthful of donut and washed it down with more coffee.

෨෬

After deciding on a day to fly over, the men headed off down the block. Naturally they carried all the unfinished donuts with them.

At the end of the block they paused, preparing to go in several directions. They were opposite a shop with a sign on the door "Antiques and Collectibles". There was an 'Open' sign on the door, but the inside of the shop was dark and gloomy. Nothing moved inside.

"You know dis one?" Francisco asked Vincent.

"Yeah, a real scumbag runs it."

"Hey, I know him too," said Greyson. "He goes around to the kupuna, buys old stuff the old people have and pays them as little as possible. Then he brings it back to his shop, puts a big price on it and sells to the tourists. I know one old lady from my church. He talked her into selling her an old lava rock poi pounder for ten dollars. Then he put it his shop window asking five hundred dollars for it. Sold it too, I think."

"Maybe we should see if he has anything in his shop that should go back to the aina like the lei niho?" Palani offered.

"Nah, too close to home. We'd get too much pilikia," said Francisco. "But sometime, maybe . . ."

The four men headed out, Palani and Greyson going different directions, Francisco and Vincent continuing straight along the sidewalk. But before they all walked away, Francisco spat on the window of the shop.

80 03

Back in a dark corner of his shop the owner, Sherman Richards, watched as the men walked away. His lip curled slightly.

"Geoffrey, get a bucket and some water. Clean the front windows . . . and the sidewalk."

Richards turned and walked into his small, dimly lit office.

A local man, dark brown from working in the sun at his other job at the Old Queen's Resort golf course, and equal in size and strength to Francisco, came from a storeroom in the back. He brought a bucket half-full with water, a squeegee and a wash rag. Opening the door, he went outside and began to clean the spit off the window.

He looked after the four men who were farther away by now.

"Francisco Na'ale, you gonna pay for making me clean this window. You gonna pay good sometime."

℠℠

A block away from the antique store, Vincent and Francisco stopped at a parked small pickup truck.

"You sure is no bother give me a ride back to my car?" Francisco asked.

"Nah, no pilikia. I gotta go back that way and stop at Longs before I go to work. Got one hot date tonight an' I need stock up . . . you know what I mean?"

Francisco flashed a wide grin.

"Sure thing, brother. Get lucky without . . . an' maybe not so lucky nine months later."

The two men got the truck and Vincent started the motor. Before pulling away from the curb he turned to Francisco.

"Hey, I been meaning to ask you. You see Koakane lately?"

Francisco's face clouded slightly.

"No. Ya know, I miss our classes. I think we were all getting pretty good at Lua. Koakane was a good teacher . . . an' we had good fun together."

"Sure, you had good fun. Good fun sitting on my back and shoving my face into the lawn."

"Well you needed to move faster . . . get away before I could grab you."

"Right. If there was more room in that yard, you'd never get me."

"Wanna bet?" Francisco said as he feinted a move at Vincent's head and punched him lightly in the stomach.

"Hey, careful, you gonna get us in an accident."

Vincent checked his side mirror and pulled out into traffic. At the next intersection he made a U-turn and headed back to where Francisco had left his truck.

❧☙

Overhead a jet's engines roared as, leaving Kona International Airport, it banked and turned toward the faraway city of Las Vegas. The 9th Hawaiian island.

7

Las Vegas

The three reels of the Megabucks slot machine spun and then, one by one, clicked and locked into position. Two cherries and a single bar sat on the center line. Mocking. Tempting.

"Well, fifteen dollars . . . better than a sharp stick in the eye."

Koakane gazed up at Teri from his seat in front of the slot machine. Then he stuck his tongue out at her.

"I think I remember somebody, now who was that, somebody who started us off and ran through her money . . . an' got nothing. Not one cherry. Not one dime back."

Teri replied by sticking her tongue back out at Koakane, and then sipping her rum and coke through the thin black straw that it had come with.

"Hey, you two, want to play tongues? Go back up to your room," Shari said. "Koakane, move it, it's mom's turn."

"I don't know," said Haunani as she moved to take over the chair from Koakane, "maybe somebody else should finish this off . . . I don't feel all that lucky."

"No way, it's your turn," Shari said, "we all agreed. We'd kick in twenty dollars each, run it through this Megabucks machine, and then split evenly all the money we get out."

"And look what we have so far," Lori said touching the machine. "Sixty dollars counting the fifteen Koakane just won. That's twelve apiece. So, mom, win big and we all get our money back."

With Lori on one side and Shari on the other Haunani was guided into the padded chair in front of the machine.

"Wait, wait," said Haunani as she shifted her large purse around to her lap.

The others all sipped at their drinks, courtesy of the Aria Hotel & Casino, which Lori had already told them, after tapping away on the screen of her cellphone, were only costing them about two hundred dollars each, "Complimentary cocktails my okole," she had said.

Haunani rummaged in her purse, bringing out Kleenex, which elicited remarks from all three sisters, "Dump those used tissues, Mom", "Yuck", "Seriously, Mom, we need to do a Spring cleaning on your purse".

Haunani paid no attention to her girls' remarks, until finally . . .

"Ahhh, there he is," she exclaimed in satisfaction.

From her purse Haunani had extracted a small plastic green frog . . . the same green as found on U.S. currency. He had a slight grin and a look in his eyes that could, possibly, be described as one of expectation.

Satisfied that she had found her lucky frog, Haunani placed him on a corner of the machine.

"He can watch over my money from there," she said.

"Yeah, yeah Mom. We all know your lucky frog. Now . . . win us some money," said Shari as she rubbed her hands together.

"Always with the money," Haunani said. "If I hadn't been there for your conception, I'd think you were part pake."

"You want me to push the button for you?" Teri asked as she reached out to the SPIN button.

Haunani slapped her hand, but lightly.

"I can do it. If I'm gonna lose money, I'll lose it myself. I don't need any help for that."

The first and second spins, at three dollars each spin, yielded nothing. On her third spin Haunani got two cherries, like Koakane had, and won fifteen dollars.

"Okay, we got seventy-five dollars in the kitty now. Just gotta get twenty-five more," Lori said.

Haunani gave her a stink eye look and turned back to the slot machine. She touched her lucky frog and pressed the SPIN button.

The reels seemed to take forever to go around and around before clicking into place.

"We won something," said Teri.

"Oh, look, two red sevens," Lori said.

"Six thousand dollars, wow," Koakane said.

The three women and Koakane all moved in and hugged Haunani while doing little jumps and dance steps. They managed not to spill any of their drinks.

A slot manager appeared as if from nowhere to congratulate Haunani and to give the group coupons for free drinks. He informed them all that before he could pay out the money, he needed to have a slot mechanic verify the wind by opening the machine.

As the slot mechanic started to open the front of the machine, Haunani stopped him.

"Wait, let me move my frog," and she reached for her lucky green frog.

But he was gone.

Look as they might none of them could find the lucky little frog anywhere on the floor around the slot machine. But the six thousand dollars in hundred dollar bills that the slot manager counted out into Haunani's hands, after the mechanic verified that the win was legitimate, made everyone feel better . . . except for Haunani who continued searching for her lucky frog.

⁐⁑

Two rows of slot machines over from the Megabucks machine a slim haole man in a lightweight blue blazer and grey slacks walked along sipping a Ginger Ale from a plastic cup. He never drank alcohol when he was working. He resisted touching the right-hand side pocket of his blazer. He knew the little green plastic frog was in his pocket. No reason to tip anyone off to its location by touching it.

As he sauntered down the aisle between two rows of slot machines his eyes roamed over the machines as if trying to decide which one to play. But his attention was primarily on the people playing those slot machines . . . and on the purses of the many women doing the playing.

Two older women caught his attention. They sat side by side in front of two dollar-slot machines. The woman on the left had a total of seven hundred and forty-four dollars in winnings already. The other woman had just over two hundred dollars in winnings.

As the man watched the woman on the right hit a three-hundred dollar jackpot. She was ecstatic as the electronic coins piled up in her bank. Her friend leaned in to watch the action on the screen . . . and a strange man leaned in between then, his arms spread around their shoulders.

"Wow, really cool, you mush be really lucky, eh Babe?"

"Pardon me," said the woman who had just won.

The man focused his attention on the woman on his right, and her slot machine screen. The noise of the coins clinking down into the bank on her screen . . . the rattle and clink of the other machines around them . . . the pressure of the man's arms on their shoulders and his too-loud voice . . . all combined so that neither woman noticed his left hand slip down and push the CASHOUT button on the machine of the woman on his left. Nor did they notice when his fingers plucked the paper CASHOUT VOUCHER strip with the seven hundred and forty-dollar total on it.

Continuing to speak the man leaned close in to the woman on his right.

"Ya know, ya could get even luckier tonight . . . maybe come upstairs with me?

The woman's friend turned toward the man and put her hand on his chest pushing him back.

"Excuse us, we wish you'd go away and leave us alone," she said.

"Excuse me," the man said straightening up and tucking the payout slip into the left side pocket of his blazer.

The man stood up and lumbered away. He turned down a crossing aisle, squared his shoulders and walked briskly away. Making his way to the elevators he got in the first one with open doors and punched the buttons for several upper level floors. After getting off on an upper floor at random he stepped into another elevator that took him back down to the floor above the casino floor. There he entered a restaurant where, once seated, he removed his blazer and laid it across the empty chair next to him. The man ordered a cappuccino and a small bowl of vanilla ice cream. Once served he savored the ice cream in small spoonfuls before slowly drinking his cappuccino. When he was halfway through with his cappuccino he reached over to his blazer and removed the little plastic green frog from the right hand side pocked, and then took the CASHOUT VOUCHER for the amount of seven hundred and forty dollars from the left hand side pocket.

"Hey, little frog, maybe you are lucky. But we won't push your luck today. We'll cash this tomorrow," and he returned both the plastic frog and the CASHOUT VOUCHER to the right side pocket of his blazer.

As he slowly drank his cappuccino, he wondered at himself. Why had he bothered with the risk of taking the plastic frog? He already knew the answer. He had done the same thing so many times before over so many years. For the thrill of it. For the rush it gave him knowing that he was taking something from somebody, and that in doing so he ran the risk of being caught. And punished.

�℈ଔ

Back on the floor the two older women were still trying to figure out how the total amount won on the one woman's machine had suddenly dropped to zero dollars.

"I know I had a lot more than that racked up," she said to her friend.

"I know you did. Did you hit some button wrong?"

"I can't have. I just can't figure it out. Shall we ask the slot manager?"

"He won't do anything. Shall we find a couple of new machines?"

"No, these have been paying good. But I think I will ask the slot manager.

And her friend was right, other than having a slot mechanic open the machine and verify that it was working correctly, the slot manager did nothing.

℘℘℘

That evening the man spread his takings for the day out on the bedspread in the forty-nine ninety-five a night motel room he was staying in. He intended to leave that room in a day or so, very early in the morning so that he didn't have to pay. The credit card he'd used at check-in wasn't even from someone in this city.

On the bedspread were three credit cards, over four hundred dollars in cash (the wallet containing the cash had long since disappeared into a trash receptacle in the men's room of another casino), the CASHOUT VOUCHER from the Aria (an errand for tomorrow) and the little green plastic frog.

"Froggie, you've been very lucky for me today," he said.

His cell phone rang as he was gathering up his day's takings.

"Yes? Uh-huh, I recognize your voice. She's coming? You're sure about this? How is she bringing her jewelry? Okay. Yes. Yes, I'll take care of that part of it. Did you tell him that I'll be bringing the merchandise and that he should pay me? Yes," he said picking up one of the credit cards from the bedspread. "I think I can afford that."

The man disconnected, put his daily 'earnings' away and decided to treat himself to a meal at a local steakhouse. He was feeling so good that he decided to actually pay for tonight's dinner.

8

Las Vegas, Sunday

Back at the Aria Hotel & Casino, the women of the Pono family, along with Koakane, had finished their main courses and were settling into their coffee and deserts. Since they were on vacation Shari assured them all that no calories they ingested would reflect on their shapely frames.

Koakane snickered at Shari's mention of 'shapely frames' and was promptly battered with napkins wielded by all of the women at the table. He apologized before they could move on to more devastating weapons, scoops of whipped cream perhaps, and the women returned to their desserts. Quiet returned to their table, except for the smacking of lips and small sighs of delight.

Shari broke that silence.

"I have an idea."

"That would be a first," Lori said, but she quickly recanted her words and raised her hands in surrender when Shari mimed flinging a scoop of her chocolate mousse onto Lori's blouse.

"We have the money we won at Megabucks, and we all have done pretty well with our personal gambling."

It was true, each of the women still held the original gambling stake they had brought with them, plus anywhere from fifty dollars to seven hundred dollars of additional winnings.

"I think we could change our plane tickets," Shari continued, "and instead of flying home tomorrow, we should fly to San Francisco. We can do some shopping and then fly home from there."

Shari's idea met with approval all around. It was decided that Lori should change their tickets since she had been the one to originally purchase them. Lori was also tasked with arranging their accommodations in San Francisco.

With that decision made, and with all the dessert dishes thoroughly cleaned, Haunani and Shari headed back to the casino floor. Lori went up to her room to make the necessary calls. And Teri, escorted by Koakane, went to catch a cab over to the California Hotel, a favorite of visiting Hawaiians, in order to shop the beef jerky store there. She had long list, added to by her sisters and her mother, of people back home who needed to be gifted with a package of beef jerky.

∞⃝∞

For their last night in Las Vegas, they all packed their suitcases, leaving out their airplane clothes and toiletries. Then Shari led them through doors and tunnels from their hotel to the one next door, where she introduced them to a really nice Chinese restaurant. The women and Koakane all ate well, they had some exotic drinks, Lori loved her chocolate martini, and then tried their luck in the casino of that hotel. Their luck held and they left with a few more coins in their pockets than they had begun with.

Teri and Koakane were the first to head upstairs. They said good night for almost ten minutes outside Teri's room. The only reason they moved apart was because Haunani arrived, proclaiming a need for sleep. Shari was the last one to turn in for the evening . . . and the last one to get up the following morning.

9

After a final trip to the breakfast buffet at the Aria, their group checked out, made their way outside and managed to find a shuttle that would hold all five of them plus their luggage. Still a little tight. Teri held one plastic shopping bag filled with packets of beef jerky of all kinds on her lap. Koakane held the second bag, similarly filled, on his lap and wondered aloud how he had gotten himself into this situation.

As the shuttle with the women and Koakane in it pulled away from the curb a good-looking man wearing a blue blazer over grey slacks stepped through the glass doors from the lobby and out into the bright sun of a Vegas day. He took a pair of expensive sunglasses from the breast pocket of his coat, put them on and, with suitcase in hand, headed over to the taxi rank. A valet signaled to a cab and the driver got out, put the man's suitcase into the trunk of the cab. The man gave the valet a dollar slot coin and got into the cab. He waited as, with a false smile, the valet closed the door of the cab all the while wishing him a safe trip home and a "Come back to visit us again". Once the door was closed on the cab, the valet stepped back, smiling still, and hissed through his teeth "Hope you fall and break your leg getting out of that cab".

ෆେ

Check-in went smoothly at MacLaren Airport and soon the women and Koakane were comfortably settled in front of a row of slot machines, their last chance to win big, not far from their departure gate.

Teri kept the two bags of beef jerky safely by her feet, touching them with her toes so as to guarantee that she would not forget them when it came time to board their plane.

A short distance away the man in the blue blazer broke one of his own rules and played a quarter slot machine. He grinned as his left hand clutched the little green frog in his pants pocket, while his right hand pushed the SPIN button on his machine. As his attention wandered around the boarding area, his machine lined up several symbols. The bells on his machine sounded and he looked back to find that he had won two hundred dollars.

Lori looked up from the machine she was playing, saw the win on the man's machine.

"Hey, good for you," she said.

"Yes," the man replied, "guess I'll leave here with a few coins in my pocket."

"Well, that's lucky," Lori said.

"Yes, lucky," the man said giving her a bright grin.

He punched the button to CASHOUT, took his voucher and headed for the cashier across the room. Still smiling he rubbed the little green frog in his pocket.

႘ၯ

When it came time to board their Southwest plane, Koakane helped Teri carry her beef jerky bags onboard and got them stowed in an overhead compartment.

The women and Koakane all settled in for the short ninety-plus minute flight to San Francisco.

Toward the back of the plane the man in the blue blazer gently touched his pants pocket, where the little green frog sat wrapped in ten new twenty dollar bills.

"Yep, lucky," the man said under his breath as the plane began taxiing toward takeoff.

10

Kona International Airport

Greyson and Vincent went through the TSA check-in with no problems. They boarded their Hawaiian Airlines flight and Greyson promptly fell asleep. Forty-two minutes later they landed in Honolulu. Vincent made a quick call on his phone, and the two men went out to wait at the curb. In only a few minutes a white Honda CRV pulled up and a woman inside waved to the two men.

"Hey, Greyson, this my baby sistah, Beatrice. Beatrice, this my friend Greyson."

"Hello, Greyson," the woman said with a welcoming smile. "So, Vincent, where do you need to go?"

"Bishop Museum, Beatrice."

"You were just there on Jeremy's field trip."

"I know, can't get enough of that place."

Beatrice shook her head, checked her rearview mirror and pulled out into the airport traffic. Greyson was glad that Vincent's sister was driving. He figured that he would have been totally lost within minutes of pulling onto the freeway.

☙❦☙

They drove down Bernice street until they saw a sign pointing the way to the Bernice Pauahi Bishop Museum. Turning off the street Greyson saw that they were in a medium-sized parking lot with buildings old and new off to one side.

"Okay, Vincent," Beatrice said, "I have to run some errands. What time do you want me to pick you up?"

"Oh, maybe two, three hours."

"Which? Two or three?"

Vincent looked to Greyson, who held up three fingers.

"Three."

"Okay, I'll be back in three hours. Stay out of trouble, brother."

"Always, sister."

Vincent and Greyson watched Beatrice pull away.

"You gonna tell her our plans?" Greyson asked.

"No way, brah. She'd spoil everything. Always thinks I don't know what I'm doing."

Greyson had his own thoughts on that subject, but kept them to himself.

The two men walked up the path toward the old building, a former Kamehameha boarding school, which was now the Hawaiian Hall and the repository of the museum exhibits.

As they walked Vincent, by virtue of his more recent visit as field trip chaperone, pointed out the large lawn area and the Science Adventure Center behind it. The two men noticed a large white tent set up in the middle of the lawn. On their right side, just before they entered the Pavilion that housed the ticket office, Vincent drew Greyson's attention to a sign that pointed the way to Café Pulama.

"Maybe after we check out the museum we can get some coffee there."

Reaching the ticket box the two men produced their Hawaiian i.d. and paid the kamaʻāina rate.

Once inside the museum they directed their attention to the three stories of the main museum portion. They looked in cases and Greyson wrote down in a small notebook that he took from his shirt pocket the number of lei niho palaoa that they saw. He noted also how many of the lei niho were on each floor. Vincent surreptitiously checked the glass doors of each exhibit, trying to determine the type of lock for each door.

Pausing on the top floor the two men leaned on the railing and looked down into the center of the museum.

"We can't take them all," Greyson said, "there's just too many for the four of us to carry out."

"Yeah," Vincent agreed, "we need to figgah out which the most important ones, an' then plan how to just get those out."

So back they went, though they started on the top floor this time. Greyson drew a map of each floor showing the approximate location of each display case that held lei niho that the two men judged to be the oldest and most important. Thus probably holding the most mana.

They judged that they had all the information they could gather today and decided to go to the café for coffee and to discuss their findings.

When Vincent and Greyson walked back down the main staircase to the bottom floor, they noticed a museum guard rocking back and forth on his heels watching a group of elementary school children as they toured the museum. The schoolchildren had a teacher and several parent chaperones with them. The teacher looked as if she had been working with children for several generations. The parent chaperones were three no-nonsense mothers. The museum guard knew from past experience that there would be no trouble from that group.

As he turned to look over another portion of the first floor exhibits, something on his shoulder peeked out from under his short sleeve shirt.

Vincent nudged Greyson, who nodded in response.

The two men stepped over to the guard.

"Hey, brah, howzit?" Vincent said.

The guard turned to the two men and gave them a wide smile.

"Is okay, but, you know, gotta stay on my toes. Nevah know when one of those gonna go ballistic an' start tearing up the place," and he indicated with a jerk of his head the group of eight and nine-year-olds gathered around their teacher as she talked about the skeleton of a honu suspended from the ceiling.

"Yeah," said Vincent, "that's some wild ones there."

Greyson observed the guard and noticed how his hat perched precariously atop his hair. The man had a gigantic head of curly red hair that could have served as a signal beacon for a Coast Guard lighthouse. His nametag read **'BUFFALO'** and with his massive head of hair and his size, a full head taller than either Vincent or Greyson, it was not hard for the men to imagine the guard as some lumbering beast.

"First time to the museum?" he asked.

"Oh, I've been here before, but this is Greyson's first time. My name is Vincent and this is Greyson. We're over from the Big Island."

"Well, hope you enjoy your visit," said Buffalo as he began to turn away.

"Actually," said Vincent, "we had some questions that maybe you could help us with?"

"Sorry, guys. My break time."

"That's okay. Maybe we could buy you a cup of coffee at the Café Pulama?"

"No more Café Pulama. Just Bishop Museum café now."

"Still got food?" Greyson asked.

"Oh, suah, not a lot of choice, but good."

"We were going there to get something to eat. How about we buy you a donut . . . or a sandwich?" said Greyson.

"Well, really not supposed to . . ."

Buffalo glanced toward the café and his tongue flicked across his lips. He nodded.

"Okay, I guess I could talk with you for a little while."

"Great," said Vincent, "an' by the way, what's that tattoo I see under your shirt on your left shoulder?"

Buffalo's hand went to his shoulder to cover the tattoo. He pulled his shirt down farther, then he seemed to reconsider. He looked around him. Then he pushed his shirt up and pointed his shoulder toward the two men.

"It's Kanaka Maoli, Hawaiian sovereignty," he said showing them the Native Hawaiian flag tattoo on his shoulder. Red and green and yellow with crossed canoe paddles over a kahili.

Buffalo pulled his shirt sleeve back down.

"Gotta be careful with tattoos. Some places you get fired for having them. Here, just gotta not make it too visible."

"That's a shame," said Vincent, "this museum should celebrate the Hawaiian sovereignty movement, not hide it."

Buffalo nodded in agreement.

"Well, said Greyson, "how about we get something to eat. Our treat, Buffalo. Our treat."

Together the three men walked over to the new Bishop Museum Café. On the way, Buffalo unclipped his belt walk-talkie and called in that he was taking his lunch break.

"Leave some food for the rest of us," his dispatcher replied.

𝕊𝕆ℂℝ

A short while later, three plates that had been filled with tako poke, poi, lau lau, hibachi chicken and rice sat empty. The three men, having refilled their large plastic soda glasses, relaxed and talked.

"So, how long you work here?" asked Vincent.

"Almos' one year now."

"Like it?" Greyson asked.

"S'okay. Steady work. Keeps my wahine off my case."

"We know how that goes," said Vincent. "What's with the big tent out on the lawn?"

"Oh, people can rent out da museum for parties and stuff. They had a big affair the other day, now they're taking it all down."

"Do those people use the museum too?"

"No, jus' the lawn. They bring in a caterer an' open the bathrooms in the Science Center. They had some big fund-raiser for something or other."

"So, they don't use the museum itself?" Greyson asked.

"No, besides, they be here on Tuesday. Museum closed on Tuesdays. But for the extra money they make the arrangements."

"Do this kinda thing often?" Vincent asked.

"Yeah, pretty often."

"They have security here for those events?"

"Just us," Buffalo said tapping the '**SECURITY**' patch on his shoulder.

"Pay extra for that?" asked Greyson.

"Oh, suah, good overtime."

"You work that kine often?" asked Vincent.

A tremble seemed to run up Buffalo's back and he shook himself to clear it away.

"Not me, not if I can help it."

"Why?"

Buffalo gazed out the window toward the museum itself.

"No like."

"Why?"

Buffalo leaned in over the table.

"That museum . . . scary place sometimes at night. The couple times I did have to work late night there . . . I could feel things. Hear things. Walking around in there, just feels . . .," he shook himself again and picked up his soda.

"You know why it's like that in there?" asked Vincent.

Buffalo shook his head.

"Because of all the things in there that the haoles stole from our people. Stole 'em and locked 'em up behind glass so that they could come look at 'em whenever they wanted."

Buffalo frowned as he contemplated this new idea.

"They stole 'em?"

"You think our Ali'i just gave all those things away? No, the haoles stole 'em. Just like they stole our land."

The three men contemplated the vision of their land and possessions being stolen over the years by haoles.

"You know," Buffalo began, "my great great grandfather was a chief over on Maui. He ruled over a big valley, over a section of Maui that reached from the mountains down to the ocean. Now, my family got nothing on Maui . . . an' all my wahine an' I got is a two-bedroom apartment we rent over in Waianae."

The men paused again to consider this injustice.

"You know, Buffalo, you and us, we the same," Vincent said. He touched the tattoo under Buffalo's sleeve. "We're all Kanaka Maoli. In fact, we're part of a group over on the Big Island working to bring sovereignty to our islands."

"And we're here today," Greyson added, "because we need your help to make that happen."

A puzzled look came over Buffalo's face as he looked from one to the other of the two men at the table with him.

"How can I help?" he asked.

Vincent and Greyson both smiled as they reached out, and both patted Buffalo on his back.

11

A server from the café had to come and tell the three men that it was past closing and he needed to shut down the café. Given the size of the three men, and the fact that one was a security guard at the museum, he was quite polite with his request. The three men moved outside and sat at a table with an umbrella in the center.

"Okay, I think I understand," said Buffalo, "I see what your group is all about. And I support you. But what you want me to do . . . that's not easy. I could lose my job, an' if I lose my job my wahine going be really mad. I mean throwing plates and cups and pots . . . and maybe even kitchen knives mad."

"There's no danger of that, Buffalo," said Vincent.

"No," Greyson said, "you told us that you can turn off the museum alarm system without entering any personal code. So there'll be no record of who turned off the alarm system. Same thing with the closed-circuit cameras. So all you have to do is shut it all down and then you, or another guard, can discover that the system is shut down and someone has been inside the museum."

"While you have been outside making sure that the party on the lawn goes along just fine," Vincent added.

"But I told you, I no like working in the museum at night. That's why I hardly ever put in for night overtime."

"But if you usually skip the night overtime, then you'll have the seniority to request it. And you can just mention that you need some extra money to buy a present for your wahine," said Vincent.

Buffalo thought for a moment.

"An' all I gotta do is turn off the alarms? No need to go into the museum, 'cuz you know is spooky in there at night."

"That's all," said Vincent, "and we'll be outta there in thirty, maybe forty minutes, tops."

"An' you're not gonna sell the things you take?"

"No, Buffalo, we're going to return them to the aina. We're going to bring the mana back to the land . . . and make Hawaii strong again."

Just then Buffalo's walkie talkie beeped.

"Buffalo? Where da frick are you? You sposed to be inside on patrol."

Buffalo grimaced before keying his walkie talkie on.

"I'm coming. Had too much kau kau and I've been in the bathroom getting rid of it."

"Too much information," came the voice over the walkie talkie. "Just get back to work."

"Ten-four," said Buffalo.

"Okay, guys, I'm in," Buffalo said to Vincent and Greyson.

"All right," said Vincent, "We'll be back on the next Tuesday when they have the big party here on the lawn. We'll check in with you right after it gets dark. Mahalo plenty, Buffalo. And malama pono da aina."

"Oh, jus' one more thing we need, Buffalo. Keys to the display cases."

That was more difficult to talk Buffalo into, but eventually he agreed.

The men stood, hugged and patted each other on the back. Then Buffalo went off to use the bathroom before going back on patrol.

Vincent and Greyson walked to the parking lot to find a very pissed-off Beatrice waiting in her car for them.

"Three hours you said! Three! Not four! Geez, Vincent, sometimes you make me so mad . . ."

"Here, Beatrice," Vincent said handing a package through the open driver side window, "bought you a present."

Beatrice opened the package.

"A tee shirt? A Bishop Museum tee shirt? I do all this for you and all I get is a lousy tee shirt?"

"Try it on later," Vincent said, "we gotta get to the airport wiki wiki an' catch our flight."

Beatrice spat out a few words at Vincent that no proper woman would ever use, but a tita would, and spun her tires kicking up gravel as she pulled out of the parking lot.

ഇൗരു

Vincent and Greyson made it onto their flight back to Hilo . . . but just barely. The Gate Agent was already starting to close the hatch to the airplane when the two men came running down the ramp. He started to wave them off, and then shook his head and pulled the hatch back open. Continuing to give the Gate Agent a thousand-watt smile, Greyson stepped through the hatch and onto the plane. Vincent frowned in puzzlement, followed Greyson and looked back at the slim Japanese Gate Agent, hair perfect, teeth perfect, just a hint of blush on his cheeks. His eyes fixed on Greyson. Vincent blinked, cocked his head to one side and filed his thoughts away for further scrutiny at some other time.

12

San Francisco

The Pono family group, accompanied by Koakane, arrived at S.F. International Airport. They retrieved their luggage, walked out to the curb and caught a van operating as a taxi into the city.

The taxi van dropped them off at Fisherman's Wharf just outside the Marriott. Lori's connections had gotten them decent rooms, at a really good price. Since it wasn't too late in the afternoon yet, the women decided to go shopping. They took a cab to Union Square and set about buying out Macy's and other stores there.

Koakane begged off from the shopping safari by claiming a headache. As soon as the women departed in their cab he set out on a walk along the piers. He watched tourists get on boats from the Red and White fleet. He watched tourists take pictures of seagulls and sea lions. He watched tourists cross the street without checking for oncoming traffic first. Generally, he just watched tourists.

His walk took Koakane all the way down to where the cruise ships docked. He stopped by one of them, *The Queen of the Islands*. Koakane recalled that this ship made regular round-trips, from San Francisco to Hawaii and back again. He wondered at the people who had enough money to afford such a trip. He decided he'd rather fly.

As he stood there looking up at the big ship and all the activity going on around it, Koakane guessed it must be getting ready to leave for the islands. His gaze was caught by two men standing by the entranceway to the ship, talking. They were near the ship, but not so near that anyone could listen in on their conversation. One man was skinny and short, probably from somewhere in the Far East. He wore a white uniform indicating to Koakane that he worked on the ship and smiled almost continuously. The other man wore a light blue sport coat and seemed somehow vaguely familiar to Koakane. The man in the uniform handed an envelope to the other man who slipped it into the inside pocket of his sport coat. They exchanged a few more words and then the man in the uniform turned and walked back toward the ship. The man in the sport coat started down the sidewalk, nodded pleasantly to Koakane as he passed him, and continued back on down toward Fisherman's Wharf.

Koakane shrugged his shoulders and decided to continue on down along the piers. He figured he had plenty of time to explore and still get in a nap before the women returned from shopping.

13

The man in the blue sport coat and the man from the cruise ship talked quietly.

"You're sure she'll be here?" the blue sport coat man said.

"Positive. She's already in the daily ship's paper for appearing in the main lounge and having dinner with the Captain. They even did a special job cleaning the suite she's going to stay in. No Norovirus for her."

"And she'll have her jewels?"

"I told you, she always brings them with her."

"Sounds okay. Now how do I get on?"

"Here," the cruise ship man said as he passed an envelope to the man in the blue sport coat. He watched as the other man slipped the envelope into the inside pocket of his sport coat. "That's your ticket for the cruise. You have an inside cabin, no porthole."

The man in the sport coat frowned.

"I could get seasick in there not being able to see outside."

"Just make sure you're okay next Tuesday when we make Hilo."

"Anything else?"

"No, get here early. The line to board gets really long. Oh, and you have to go through metal detectors."

"No problem."

"All right, see you on board tomorrow. Your cabin is on my work schedule so there won't be any suspicion about my stopping by now and then."

The two men turned and walked away from each other.

As he walked back toward Fisherman's Wharf, the man in the blue sport coat smiled to himself thinking about the successful conclusion of his next heist. He nodded to a dark-skinned man who stood watching the ships before continuing on to his motel room where he would memorize his cruise ticket and the information on it.

It looked to be a profitable cruise.

14

Koakane was enjoying a nice nap in his room at the Sheraton Fisherman's Wharf Hotel. He decided it was good that Lori had all those connections with hotel people here and there and around the world. *Maybe Teri and I should take a trip . . . just the two of us. Maybe to some place like Fiji. That might be nice and maybe we could . .*

Koakane's thoughts were interrupted by the ringing of the phone beside his bed. He rolled over, fumbled for the phone and finally got it to his ear.

"Hello?"

"What? Sleeping?" said Shari.

"What for you want to wake me up? Don't you know I have to get my rest?"

"Rest for what? You don't even make-out with my sister, much less do anything you gotta rest up from . . ."

A shriek came over the phone and Koakane heard signs of a struggle.

"Hello, Koakane? Don't listen to my rude sister," said Teri.

Koakane rolled onto his back with the phone to his ear and smiled.

"Now you know, Teri, maybe she has a point there."

"The only point my rudest sister has is on top of her head. We're back from shopping and we're hungry. Come on over to my room and we'll decide where to go."

Teri hung up and Koakane made his way to the bathroom to make himself presentable. As he combed his hair he returned to his thoughts.

Yeah, just the two of us, no sisters, no mother. Just the two of us at some nice resort down in Fiji. Nice and warm with no one else around.

Koakane wondered if he had time for a quick cold shower.

15

Teri answered the door to the room she shared with Lori. Haunani had chosen to share a room with Shari, as she was the only one who could keep her under some kind of control.

Teri gave Koakane a quick kiss on the lips, and took his hand guiding him into the room.

Shari started to do a 'Whoop Whoop' upon seeing Teri's kiss, but cut it off upon receiving a stink-eye look from Haunani.

"Oh, Lord!" Koakane exclaimed as he saw all the shopping bags and their contents strewn about the room.

"We never going to get all this on the plane!" he said gesturing wide with his arms.

"You'll figure something out," Lori said, "but right now we're hungry."

Koakane continued to survey the results of the women's shopping safari and mentally calculated the tips involved for bell hops and valets. But he also thought back to previous trips to San Francisco.

"How about Castagnola's? Not a long walk and really good food. Nice place to eat at the Wharf."

The women all agreed and within ten minutes they had cleaned up the room, and themselves, and were heading out of the lobby bound for Castagnola's.

It was a short walk from their hotel to the famous Fisherman's Wharf restaurant. The lights were on both inside and outside, welcoming one and all. Once through the front door, a maitre'd greeted them, asked the size of their party and led them through the restaurant toward a table by the windows that looked out onto the fishing boats that plied the Bay during the day.

They had almost reached their table when . . .

"Hey, Aloha Haunani, how you doing?"

Next to their table was another table with six women sitting around it. The oldest of the woman, who looked to be in her seventies, got up from her chair, stepped over and put her arms around Haunani.

"Girl, you look so good," the woman said.

"Honey, you look fantastic. How long since we got together?"

"Too long, dear. Way too long. You know my daughters?" Honey asked pointing to the women at the table. Three of the women, middle-aged, waved at Haunani and her party.

"And my granddaughters?"

The two youngest women at the table smiled and said "Hello" "Aloha" and "Nice to see you Auntie".

All six of the women were decked out in bright blouses and wore necklaces and Hawaiian bangle bracelets. Honey had so many gold bracelets that they looked as if they might drag her arm down into the salad when she ate.

"So, what are you doing here?" Honey asked.

"We're on our way home from Vegas," Shari put in. "What about all of you?"

"We're getting ready to take the cruise ship back to Hawaii," Honey said.

"We were until now," said one of Honey's daughters.

"Were?" said Shari stepping up beside her mother and Honey.

"Sit, sit," said Honey. "It's a long story."

Haunani and her daughters, along with Koakane, took seats at their table. Teri maneuvered to sit next to Koakane, noting as she did so the looks he got from all the women at the other table.

A waiter came and took drink orders, and once that was taken care of Honey began telling her story.

ಬಂಛ

Honey and her daughters and granddaughters performed regularly on the cruise ship *The Queen of the Islands*. They were a hula group based in Hilo. In addition to their rooms and their meals, the cruise line paid them for their performances. They alternated with another group from O'ahu, performing for a month and then taking a month off.

Honey had just gotten bad news from the Big Island. Her husband had gone in to the emergency room of the local hospital and then had been transferred to Kona Community Hospital. His problem was yet undiagnosed.

Honey and her troupe would have to leave for Hilo.

"Today, about six hours from now. We're all packed. Cruise line not too happy with us, but what can we do. Taking a red-eye home."

"More important for you to get home to be with your husband," said Haunani who had lost her husband many years ago.

A cloud of silence settled over the two tables. To be broken by Koakane.

"What about if Haunani and her daughters took over for you?"

"What?" said Honey and Haunani at the same time.

Koakane turned to Lori.

"Are our plane tickets refundable?"

"Yes."

"We don't need the money that the cruise line pays, do we?"

All the women at his table agreed to that.

"Are we in a big hurry to get home?"

They weren't. In fact, Shari was delighted at the prospect since she'd never been on a cruise before.

"Okay," said Koakane, "so Lori calls her hotel and says she's gonna take a few more days off. And she gets us what's left of our airline tickets back. Honey and her Hilo Honies get over to the Big Island and check out her husband's condition. If he's okay, then when the ship gets to Hilo, she and her girls get back onboard to finish out the cruise. We get off there, rent a car and drive on home. Simple, yah?"

Honey agreed and the deal was made. It only had to be confirmed by a phone call from Honey to the Recreation Director on the ship.

"We're all good to go," Honey said as she ended the call. "You can have our staterooms. We leave our hula gear on board the ship in storage so you can use that. I'll even give you a video to watch of one our performances so you'll know how our act goes."

The only objections came from Teri and Lori and Haunani.

"But I haven't danced in years," said both Teri and Lori.

"I'm too old for this," said Haunani.

"It'll come back to you really easily," said Honey to the two girls, "And you're as young as ever," she lied to Haunani.

With the cloud of gloom mostly lifted, both tables settled down to enjoy their San Francisco dinner. Since they were at Fisherman's Wharf, the dinner choice was for fresh crab all around.

The talk went back and forth as Haunani and her girls tried to learn as much as possible about the show they would be performing. Koakane was less than elated when it was pointed out to him that, since it was his idea, he would be performing also.

"But no fire knife dance," Honey said. "The Captain doesn't want you burning his ship up."

"An' we don't have a costume for you," one of Honey's daughters said.

"That's okay," Shari said, "We'll make him a malo out of a ship's towel."

Shari blinked her eyes ingenuously as Koakane growled at her.

Teri repressed a smile from behind her wine glass.

✼

Once they were finished with dinner, Honey and her Hilo Honies called for a shuttle van to take them back to the ship to collect their luggage and then on to the airport to catch their flight to the Big Island.

While they waited for the shuttle van, hugs and kisses were exchanged over and over again. The shuttle van arrived.

"Okay, Haunani, see you all next Tuesday," Honey said giving Haunani one last hug.

"Next Tuesday?" said Koakane.

"Sure. That's when the ship pulls into Hilo for the day."

"Oh, right."

Haunani and her newly-formed hula troupe waved as Honey and the Hilo Honies pulled away from the curb in the shuttle van.

As the van turned the corner, Haunani, her girls and Koakane began their stroll back to the Sheraton. They stopped to pick up a few final Fisherman's Wharf souvenirs along the way. Arriving at the hotel they all soon found that the wonderful dinner, combined with the stroll along the docks, had prepared them perfectly for a good night's sleep. Which is exactly what they had.

16

Kona

"Okay, we're set for next Tuesday," Vincent said. "Everybody gotta get one plane ticket for Honolulu. When we get to the museum turn off your phone. Buffalo said he would get the CC TV cameras turned off, but just to be safe we all gonna wear bandanas."

The men were seated around a table at their favorite coffee house in Kona. After glancing around the room to assure himself that no one was taking an undue interest in their activities, Vincent pulled four newly printed black bandanas from a paper sack and passed them around. Across the front they had the group's motto printed in yellow, *Malama Pono O Ka `Āina.*

Vincent made them all practice tying on the bandanas until he was sure none of them would fall off.

"Put 'em in your pockets," he said, "an' remembah, they not for blowing your nose." He looked directly at Francisco as he said this last bit.

"One more thing," Vincent said as he pulled up a large shopping bag from under the table. He opened the bag and took out four folded plastic carry-on bags. Holding one bag open he showed the others the lettering on it. It read *Hawaiian Independent Films – Prop Department.* "When you collect the lei niho that you're assigned, put them in the bag. Then, when you get to the airport if anyone stops you, you tell 'em that these are props for a film being made on-island. You tell 'em that they're plastic with artificial hair."

"And here," Vincent continued as he handed each of the others a sheet of paper. "Peel-off labels," the men all looked at the labels on the paper, they read Property of *Hawaiian Independent Films*. "Stick 'em on the backside of each lei niho. That should convince any suspicious gate agent."

The men put their bandanas and the sheets of peel-off labels into the plastic carry-on bags.

The four men stood, extended their hands and placed them one over the other so that they were linked. Then, solemnly, they murmured so that no one should overhear them . . . "Imua, Lanakila."

They left the café with determination showing on their faces, and purpose in their stride.

17

San Francisco, Cruise Ship Terminal

The shuttle van driver was somewhat displeased at the short run from the Sheraton to the Cruise Ship Terminal. The smile returned to his face when Koakane over-tipped him.

Koakane left the women at the curb and returned a few minutes later with a porter and a luggage trolley. Their luggage filled the trolley completely. The porter started in one direction, but, when informed that they were joining the ship's company as entertainers, turned and led them in another direction.

Their group did not have to go through a metal detector, as all the regular passengers did, but they did have to meet with the cruise ship Recreation Director, produce identification and sign a contract spelling out their duties and remuneration for the cruise. Then they were turned over to a ship's cabin steward, a short man, fairly skinny but wiry. His hair was fast disappearing and he kept it combed to one side and slicked down with pomade. Koakane guessed that he was originally from some island in the Pacific.

After collecting smart cards that would unlock their cabins and also track them as they left or returned to the ship, the cabin steward led their group through the ship starting by way of some back elevators designated for **CREW USE ONLY**. He pushed the luggage trolley ahead of them into the elevator, and Teri stopped herself from remarking that had the cabin steward not been so skinny, they all would not have fit.

Teri thought that they were going to wind up deep in the bowels of the cruise liner, all crushed together into one small cabin. She was surprised and pleased when the cabin steward led them up to a very high deck and showed them the three cabins allotted to their group.

Haunani kept Shari with her and took the first cabin, a mini-suite with a nice little balcony, two twin beds and a bathroom with a shower and tub. Lori and Teri took the twin to Haunani and Shari's cabin, also with a balcony and twin beds. Their cabins were side by side.

Koakane, with his luggage, was deposited in a cabin across the corridor and several cabins down. His was an interior cabin and as such had no balcony or porthole. He did have a queen bed and a bathroom all to himself, but he wondered how he would find his way around his cabin once he turned off the lights. His solution was that he left the light in the bathroom on around the clock, and the light spilling out under the closed door was sufficient for him to maneuver in the dark.

The cabin steward removed the rest of the group's luggage from the luggage cart and, at Haunani's direction, placed it all in her and Shari's cabin.

As he removed the luggage he noticed the large shopping bags from Las Vegas, with many bags of beef jerky in them.

"Ohhh, for me?" he said.

"Sorry, ummmm," Teri said. "Presents for the folks back home."

"My name is Rosario," the cabin steward said as he finished explaining the working of each cabin to the group. "You put this little tag," he took the tag from a plastic pocket on the inside of the door as he spoke, "and put it here where your cabin key goes. So you turn it this side up if your cabin needs service. Or you turn it the other side up if you want privacy."

Koakane and Teri both contemplated the possibilities that the little tag offered.

Koakane slipped the cabin steward a twenty-dollar bill.

"Oh, that's not necessary, sir," said Rosario as he slipped the bill into the front pocket of his jacket. "Tipping is not required onboard during the cruise."

"I'm sure we'll need you to help us with something extra during the cruise," Koakane said.

Rosario inclined his head in a small bow to the group.

"Just call me on the phone in your cabin if you need anything," Rosario said as he backed out of the door to Haunani's cabin. He closed the door behind him leaving the group alone to discuss their new accommodations.

ಶಿೇ

"Well, what shall we do first?" Lori asked.

"Let's watch the dvd that Honey gave Mom," Shari said.

It took them a few minutes to find the dvd, finally located in the bottom of Haunani's purse, and then a few minutes more to figure out how to operate the dvd player part of the tv.

They watched a whole show of *Honey and her Hilo Honies* and then sat, saying nothing, for a full minute.

Unable to take the strain any longer, Shari broke the silence.

"Damn, they're good!"

"Think we can really fill in for them?" asked Lori.

"I don't know," said Shari.

"Oh, come on girls, you just need some practice time. It'll all come back," Haunani encouraged them.

"Besides, you got one thing Honey doesn't have," said Koakane.

"What's that?" asked Teri.

"Me!" said Koakane pulling open his shirt to reveal his toned abs.

When the women were done laughing, they had to admit that Koakane, even without his fire knife routine, could dance a mean hula.

"An' lots of old women on this cruise. We better circle 'round you an' guard you off the stage when the show's over," said Shari.

They all agreed though, that some practice was necessary. Haunani called the Recreation Director and found a time when the showroom was empty so that they could practice. With his help she also located the storage area where the Honie's troupe costumes were kept, along with a boom box and cd's of the songs they would be dancing to.

The group split up. Lori and Teri moved their luggage from Haunani's cabin to their own. Teri put her plastic bags with the beef jerky packages in one corner of the room. The women in the two cabins set about unpacking and refreshing themselves. Once that was accomplished they all set off together to find their way to the showroom.

18

Rosario went about his business for the day, but checked on the long line of boarding passengers frequently. When he saw the man in the blue sport coat getting close to actually coming onboard, Rosario made his way down to the area where the man would enter. Rosario waited and stepped forward just as soon as the man had his room card swiped and had been welcomed aboard.

"Here, sir, I show you to your cabin," Rosario said as he led the man away.

No words were spoken between the two men until they were inside the man's cabin with the door closed behind them.

"Kinda small, Rosario."

"Just be thankful that this guy," Rosario glanced at his clipboard, "Ted Brinder, got sick at the last moment. I was able to keep him on the passenger roster and he won't know a thing about it until he gets his VISA bill next month. And when he disputes it, he'll find that not only was he on the ship but that he ran up charges for the bar, special dining, and the gift shop. So, now you're Ted Brinder."

"But I'm still J.J. when no one's around, Rosario. When does my luggage get here?"

"An hour, maybe less, maybe more. They'll deliver it here. You could go out, check out the ship. We really lucked out. Her suite is on this same deck."

J.J. turned away from his examination of the television and the mini-bar.

"So we're sure then?"

"Yes. She probably won't board until later, but she'll be here in time to dine with the Captain."

"And her room is on this deck?"

"Yes, her *cabin* is all the way up at the end of the corridor and straight ahead."

"Her jewels?"

"Never travels without them. Only wears them for special occasions, like tonight for the Captain's dinner, but she'll have them with her."

"And she uses the room safe?"

"Yes. I guess she figures that it's safe since she can set the combination."

"No one ever told her that there's a way into those safes if someone goes off and leaves them closed?"

"I guess not. Or maybe she's just so used to having everything go the way she wants that she's never bothered to worry about it."

J.J. took a mineral water out of the mini-bar, opened it and poured some into a glass. He sipped a little and thought.

"And our first stop is still Honolulu?"

"Yes," said Rosario as he poured the rest of the mineral water into another glass which he drank from. "They're trying a new route for some reason. Starting with O'ahu and finishing up at Maui."

"Whatever," J.J. said, "I won't be with them after Hilo. And that's Tuesday, so Monday night we pull this off after we leave Honolulu."

For a minute the two men sized each other up, neither one entirely trusting the other in this venture.

"So," said J.J., "who's this guy that's going to buy the jewels from us?"

"He's an antiques dealer in Kona. His name is Sherman Richards."

"Sounds like he should sell pianos," J.J. said and they both laughed.

"Only if they were stolen," Rosario replied.

"How do you know him?" J.J. asked.

Rosario's brow wrinkled as he thought about his answer.

"I meet him a few years back. Before I start working the cruise line. I got hired on as . . . kind of a waiter, helper, for this catamaran outfit in Honolulu. It was a private catamaran. You had to join the group, pay a fee, and then you could go out with them on weekly sailings. The catamaran was called *The Mahu Kai*. Really pretty, all pink with green and yellow highlights."

Rosario was quiet for a moment.

"I think I heard that mahu means queer?" said J.J.

"Yeah, in Hawaiian can mean you go both ways. Like I said, was a very private group. I worked there for a few months, then they got some bad publicity and had to shut down. Sold the catamaran for pennies because of its history. But I met Mr. Williams on it and he told me if I ever had anything good that I wanted to sell quietly, I should call him. So, when I found out about this woman and her jewelry, I called him. An' he's eager to buy."

"But at only forty percent of value."

"Yes, but that's still a lot of money. An' like he says, he has to take the risk of selling her stolen jewelry."

"Yeah, but we still take on the risk of stealing it . . . and getting off the boat with it."

"No worries, she probably won't even know it's gone until we're long gone. Besides, this risk is worth it."

J.J. nodded.

"You're right. A few days from now we'll have a whole lot more money in our pockets. Here's to an easy heist."

The two men clinked glasses, following which Rosario left the cabin and went back to welcoming passengers onboard and delivering them to their cabins. J.J. used the bathroom facilities and then set out to explore the ship. *You never know what someone might just leave lying around for anyone to pick up*, he thought as he consulted the small ship's map for the quickest route to the on-board casino.

19

Haunani and her 'troupe' made their way through the ship and eventually located the *Aloha Lounge* where they would perform nightly, beginning the next night. They brought with them water bottles from the mini-bar in Haunani's cabin.

"All right," Haunani said, "we have tonight off, so we need to check out all our costumes and instruments before we run through the show we're going to put on tomorrow."

Since the lounge was empty they were able to pull all of the gear left by *Honey's Hilo Honies* out onto the stage and sort through it. They sorted through the costumes and found ones for each of the women. By chance they turned up material that could be used to provide Koakane with a malo. While Koakane sat on the edge of the stage sewing his costume, the women hauled out ukuleles and drums and gourds and practiced playing those instruments. Shari found a boom box and the connection to the lounge's sound system. She also found a small box of cd's, most of them having been cut with only one song. That made it much easier to play the accompaniment to a dance.

The troupe spent the next two hours playing the cd's and practicing various hula dances. Teri roughed out a script for their performance, using some of what they had seen on the dvd Honey had left them, and using some of what they did back at their own luau at home. Koakane wound up with three individual numbers, but balked at dancing *Ke Kali Nei Au,* the *Hawaiian Wedding Song,* with Teri as Shari suggested.

"Okay," Shari said, "so skip that song. But maybe use a little less fabric in your malo . . . you know, give the old girls in the audience a little something to remember you by."

Koakane used an extra Tahitian dance skirt to snap Shari with. She retaliated with some water from her bottle. The others joined in and only stopped when Lori slipped in some of the spilled water on the stage.

"Enough!" Hauani said. "You get stupid an' someone going to get hurt."

Teri checked her watch.

"How about we stow all this gear and come back tomorrow after breakfast to practice some more?" she said.

"And after we pack this all away, we could go get some dinner. I'm starved," Shari said.

They carried everything back to the dressing room behind the stage, hung up their costumes and put away the boom box, musical instruments and cd's.

They stopped before exiting the lounge and looked back at the empty stage.

"We can do this, girls," Haunani said.

"Sure we can," said Lori, "besides what's the worst they could do to us if we flop?"

"Make us swim home?" said Shari.

Koakane held the door open as the women exited on their way to the main dining room.

But as he closed the door behind them, Koakane saw a poster taped to the inside of the window to the lounge. He frowned. His face grew hard, and his eyes flashed. But he decided to say nothing to the others, at least not right now.

20

The Captain, the First Mate and the Recreation Director were all gathered to meet their celebrity guest as she boarded the ship. The movie star/celebrity/rich person was Marilyn Hardin. Though her days playing the sexy lead in adventure films were long gone, she still attempted to portray that persona. She was dressed in a pantsuit, tailored to enhance the curves she still maintained through rigorous exercise, usually carried out in time with the fitness video that she had made many millions from. Her pantsuit was beige and its jacket cut in at her waist. Diamonds dripped from her fingers and wrist while chocolate Tahitian pearls encircled her neck. The pearls served also to keep anyone from noticing the slight wrinkles that had returned after her last plastic surgery. She was stunning, and she knew it.

"Ms. Hardin, I'm Captain Rivera. And this is my First Mate, Mr. Osteroff and our Recreation Director, Mr. Wilkerson. It's my pleasure to welcome you aboard *The Queen of the Islands.*" He extended his hand.

Taking his hand gracefully in her own, Marilyn Hardin flashed a thousand-watt smile that almost made Captain Rivera revert to adoring schoolboy status. He was so smitten that he barely noticed the crowsfeet at the corner of Marilyn's eyes, or the slight crepe around her neck. Her last facelift was wearing off and Marilyn had plans to undergo another procedure after she got off the ship and before returning to the mainland.

"Thank you so much, Captain, or should I say 'Mahalo'. But I have traveled on this ship before and I do remember all of you," Marilyn said with a lingering look at the six foot four frame of the First Mate. Mr. Osteroff was composed enough not to blush, though his mind was fixed on the previous cruise Ms. Hardin had taken with this ship.

"You know I'll be getting off in Maui? I have friends there that I plan to stay with for a month or so."

"Yes," the Captain said, "that won't be any problem at all. We do wish you could complete the whole voyage with us, but we are delighted with the time you will spend with us. You do know that our itinerary has changed for this trip and we will stop at Maui last?"

"Oh, yes, I'm well aware of the new itinerary. I will enjoy visiting the other islands before I disembark."

"Very good," said the Captain, "now, if you'd like to see your cabin?"

"That would be delightful. It's been a hectic morning and I think a short rest would do me good."

Turning away the Captain picked out Rosario hovering a few steps away.

"Rosario."

"Yes, Captain."

"Please escort Ms. Hardin and her luggage to her cabin."

"Yes, Captain."

Rosario stepped around to take hold of a luggage cart, one almost groaning under the weight of the suitcases on it. He extended one hand toward the small bag that Ms. Hardin carried herself. She pulled the bag back a little.

"Oh, no thank you. I prefer to keep this bag with me."

So would I, Rosario thought, *with all that lovely jewelry in it.*

"If you would just follow me, madam," Rosario said and he walked toward the elevators. Rosario bowed Ms. Hardin into the elevator then stepped in himself and pulled the luggage cart in. He pushed the button for an upper floor and smiled as the doors closed and the elevator rose.

℘℘

As the three men watched Ms. Hardin walk away, the Recreation Director, Mr. Wilkerson, spoke to the Captain out of the corner of his mouth.

"Why do we have her on board, Captain? And with a free suite?"

"I believe the CEO of the company has some . . . interest in her."

"Ohhh, and he wants to get that interest . . . rewarded?"

"Mmm hmm."

The First Mate had been listening to the quiet conversation between the other two men.

"She's still a fine looking woman," he said.

The Captain slowly turned his head and looked directly at the First Mate. A slow smile came across his face.

"Well, I'll defer to you on that," the Captain said. "After all, I believe you have much more *intimate* knowledge than either of us."

The blush returned to the First Mate's cheeks, but he still smiled and said, "That I do, Captain. That I do."

21

Marilyn Hardin barely noticed the older woman, dark-skinned from years of Hawaiian sun, who stood in her doorway as Rosario pushed the luggage trolley up the corridor.

She didn't see the older woman look after them for a minute before stepping back into her cabin and closing the door.

ᏚᏣ

"Here we are, Ma'am," Rosario said holding the door to her cabin open for Marilyn.

She walked past him into the cabin and he followed with the luggage trolley.

"Where would you like your luggage?"

"Oh, put it in the bedroom. Leave the two big suitcases on the bed so I can unpack them."

"Yes, Ma'am."

Rosario unloaded the luggage trolley and placed everything in the bedroom of the suite. Marilyn stopped him several times in order to have him place items where they would be more convenient for her to unpack. Rosario began to explain the various workings of the lights and all in the suite, but Marilyn stopped him.

"I've been here before, I remember how things work," she said.

"Yes, Ma'am," Rosario said maneuvering the luggage trolley out of the door of the suite.

"Oh, would you like me to put that bag away for you?" he asked pointing to the small bag Marilyn had carried into the room and had deposited on a chair.

"No, thank you. I'll put this away myself," she said glancing toward the bedroom area of the suite as if she could actually see the room safe from where she stood.

Rosario smiled tightly at the glance Marilyn made.

"The safe is in the closet, Ma'am," he said.

Marilyn's head whipped around but she relaxed as she looked upon the thin, slightly balding wisp of a cabin steward with the innocuous smile standing just inside the doorway to the cabin.

"Yes, thank you, I remember."

"If you need anything during the cruise, Ma'am, just ring me on the phone," he said indicating the phone on the long table against the cabin wall.

"Yes, I will," Marilyn said. She turned her back on Rosario and surveyed her suite.

After a brief pause, Rosario gave a slight shrug to his shoulders, pushed the trolley all the way out into the hall and let the door close behind him.

Rosario spat lightly onto the carpet at the doorway.

"Cheap bitch," he said, "keep your jewelry safe . . . for now."

He rolled the luggage trolley back down the corridor while checking his pager for messages.

₮₧

With the door to her suite closed, Marilyn Hardin relaxed. She took off the jacket she wore and unbuttoned the top button of her pants. Carrying her small bag Marilyn stepped into the bedroom area of her suite and opened the closet door. There was the safe. It swung open and she quickly reviewed the instructions from the sticker on the front of the door. Tapping in her own combination, one that held a good deal of sentimental value, she opened and closed the door twice in order to be sure it was working correctly.

Then she opened her small bag and proceeded to remove a number of small drawstring jewelry bags. She placed six bags, each containing one of her dramatic rings, some set with diamonds some set with pearls, in the safe. She put three more bags, each containing either a heavy gold bracelet or green jade bracelet, into the safe. Then she put two bags that held necklaces carefully on top of the other bags. Lastly she removed the chocolate Tahitian pearls from around her neck, placed them in the safe, then slipped off her diamond bracelet and set it in the safe beside her pearls. A carved opal ring and a large solitaire diamond ring followed.

Marilyn closed the safe and watched the indicator show 'Locked'. She breathed deeply, secure once more in the knowledge that her precious jewelry was safe again. She marveled at the knowledge that such a small safe held over two million dollars in jewelry now. Jewelry that she had accumulated through marrying two extremely wealthy men, as well as allowing herself to be romanced by several others.

22

Having finished their dinner in the very beautiful Italian restaurant several decks down from their cabins, the workout of their practice session along with the pasta and wine they had all downed combined to produce a chorus of yawns.

"I think maybe I could use a little nap, right after I finish unpacking," Haunani said.

"I second that," said Lori.

The five of them stood and, after thanking their waiter and the maitre'd, walked toward the door to the restaurant. At the door Haunani, Lori and Shari turned left toward the elevators. Teri and Koakane stopped and stood in the hallway, streams of passengers passed by them.

Haunani and her two daughters stopped also and looked back. Haunani cocked her head to one side.

"Coming?"

Teri looked over at Koakane.

"I think we're going to take a walk around outside, on the deck. Look at the ocean for a while."

Haunani nodded.

"Okay, we'll see you later," she said.

Lori and Haunani turned away and resumed their trek to the elevators. Shari paused a moment more, grinned at her sister and

Koakane. She turned to follow Lori and Haunani, but not before she said, "Be good you two . . . and maybe do something I might do." She gave a little throaty chuckle and walked away.

Teri and Koakane watched the other three walk down the hallway. Koakane took Teri's hand.

"I think the doors to the Promenade Deck are over that way," he said as he led Teri in the opposite direction from the elevators.

₧)₩

Haunani and her two daughters made their way through the ship, marveling at everything and making mental notes to return later in the voyage to check on this or that. They waited for the elevator to take them to their floor. Though Haunani counted eight elevators, it seemed that the one they wanted was always full or its doors closed just before they could make their way through the crush of people also waiting for an elevator.

Finally they were able to squeeze into an elevator, bright and shiny with loads of mirrors on the inside. The other people in the elevator were polite, but it was still difficult getting out through all those bodies.

They turned the wrong way at first, but quickly reversed direction and found their way to their cabins. The women spent the next half hour hanging and folding their clothes. Just as Shari hung up her last blouse, the doorbell to their cabin rang. Haunani stepped over to the door and let Lori in. As Lori came in, Haunani leaned out to look down the corridor. No sign of either Kokane or Teri. She closed the door behind her and sat down on the sofa.

While the women reviewed their day and talked about their plans for tomorrow, Haunani glanced repeatedly at the cabin door, willing the bell to ring and announce Teri's return. Once she had even stepped over to the door, opened it and looked out. All she saw however was the cabin steward, Rosario, pushing a heavily loaded luggage trolley along while some overly dressed older haole woman followed behind.

23

Out on the Promenade Deck, Teri and Koakane walked until they found an unoccupied spot along the railing. They leaned on the railing and breathed the salt air as they watched the foam from the ship's passage fall away quickly behind them. They didn't talk for a long time. During that time the other passengers left the deck in small groups preferring the comfort of the ship's interior to the cool breeze outside.

After a time Koakane turned and leaned his left side against the rail and looked steadily at Teri.

"What?" she said.

Koakane smiled, leaned over and kissed Teri lightly on her lips. He pulled back slightly, and Teri followed with her own kiss on his lips.

"Let's go up to my cabin," Koakane said.

"A much better choice than mine," said Teri, "I don't think Lori brought earplugs with her."

"Going to be like that?" Koakane said.

"Maybe," Teri said with an impish smile.

Koakane put an arm around Teri's shoulder and she slid her arm around his waist. They set off to find the nearest elevators.

24

Haunani decided to check once more and opened the door to look down the corridor again.

She saw the 'Do Not Disturb' tag in the lock of Koakane's cabin. She took one step out intending to knock on Lori and Teri's cabin . . . but pulled back. What if Teri was not in *her* cabin? Haunani thought for a moment and decided she didn't need to know . . . nor did it really matter.

In fact, she thought, *that might be a good thing and this might be a good place for a new beginning.*

Haunani stepped back into her cabin and softly closed the door behind her.

I could use a nap, she thought.

୫୬ଔ

Teri came out of the bathroom guided by the light shining under the bathroom door. She stepped over to the bed and pulled the covers back. She paused.

"Something the matter?" Koakane asked from where he lay in the bed.

"I thought . . . I thought I heard a door close."

"Maybe the bathroom door behind you."

"No . . . no it sounded like it was out in the hall. And it felt like someone was watching me . . . before the door closed."

Koakane braced himself up on his elbow.

"Nobody here but you an' me. An' I locked our door an' put that tag thingie in the slot on the outside. So, how about coming to bed before you get all cold out there?"

Teri slid into the bed.

"Better, huh?" said Koakane.

"Much."

"Okay, let's see just how much better we can get."

25

Francisco's cellphone rang. He looked at the screen and recognized the caller. Sergeant Akamai. He took a deep breath and answered the call.

"Aloha."

"Francisco, we talked about this earlier. The date's firmed up. I need you that night. Okay?"

"Uhhh, I do have something else I'm s'posed to do . . . over on O'ahu that night."

"Cancel it. You belong our group now. This is your first time. It's important."

Francisco took another deep breath and thought about the step he was taking.

"Francisco?"

"Yeah, I'm here. What time do we meet and where?"

The sergeant told him.

ೞೞ

"Yeah?" Vincent said as he answered his cellphone.

"Vincent, it's me . . . Francisco."

"Hey, howzit Francisco. What you want?"

There was a pause as Francisco gathered his thoughts on the other end of the phone.

"Well, I got some bad news."

Another pause.

"So, what's your bad news," Vincent asked.

"I cannot do it."

"Cannot do what?"

"The thing . . . the thing we been planning."

It was Vincent's turn to pause.

"Vincent? Vincent? You hear me?"

"You mean you no can come with us? You no can be a part of this? Why?"

Vincent clearly heard Francisco swallow before he replied.

"It's . . . ummm, it's personal. It's just . . . personal."

"You gonna tell me?"

"I cannot . . . it's just something personal that I can't get away from."

"You know this makes it mo' difficult for the rest of us? No time get someone else into our group to help. With only three of us we can not take so much. Are you sure, Francisco? Are you sure you can't find a way to be with us on this?"

"No, sorry Vincent. I hate to do this, but I no can help with this."

"Okay, Francisco. I'll tell the others. An' then we'll need to decide on your status with the group."

"Uhh, I understand. I don' wan' to leave the group. Jus' this thing, I cannot do this. I'm sorry, Vincent. I'm sorry."

Vincent heard the phone hang up on Francisco's end. He looked at his cellphone for a little bit before ending the call. He thought for a moment and then scrolled through his contacts menu to find the phone numbers of Palani and Grayson. He dialed Palani first.

₧₧

"Sergeant Akamai."

"It's Francisco."

"Oh, Francisco. What do you want?"

"I'm gonna be free to meet with you that night."

"Good. I'll call you a couple days before and go over what you need to bring with you."

"Okay."

"You sound a little down."

"Yeah, just a little. Had to break an engagement to make the meeting."

"Well, that's part of what you're taking on. You okay with that?"

"Yeah, I'm fine."

"Okay, I'll call you."

Both men hung up. Sergeant Akamai went back to the stack of paperwork on his desk. Francisco got himself a beer from the kitchen, sat back down on his couch and did some heavy thinking.

℘)(℞

On the ship Rosario dialed a '9' and then entered an outside number.

"Yes?" said a soft oily voice.

"She's on the ship and her jewels are with her."

"Good. Things look okay?"

"Yeah, J.J.'s a weasel, but I've dealt with weasels before."

"Keep an eye on him."

"Don't worry, I can take care of myself. Just make sure you have the money when J.J. gets there."

"You're not coming?"

"No, I worry might be too suspicious for me to leave the ship just then. J.J. will pick up our money, an' then I'll leave the ship in Maui and catch up with him and we'll split it.   I'm not hanging about on the island."

"Tell him to bring the jewels and I'll have the money waiting."

"Good," said Rosario as he hung up.

℘)(℞

Over in Kona, Sherman Richards terminated his end of the call. He stood, mentally reviewing the steps to take once he had the jewels in his possession.

"What you wan' me do now?"

Richards jumped away from the gigantic dark man who had suddenly materialized beside him. He relaxed his hand in his jacket side pocket, the one where he kept a small .32 semi-automatic pistol.

"God damn it, don't do that," he roared. As the man opened his mouth to speak Richards continued, "I have told you and told you, don't sneak up on me like that. You're goddamn scary enough as it is with that face of yours, I don't need you surprising me."

"Sorry," Geoffrey said hanging his head.

"Go clean the storeroom, it's filthy," Richards said, more softly now that his heart wasn't beating so fast.

"Sure thing, boss," Geoffrey said as he turned toward the back of the antique store. Richards couldn't see Geoffrey's face turned as he was. Thus he missed seeing Geoffrey's nasty smile.

Gotcha again, you mahu bastard, he thought.

26

"Everything okay?" J.J. asked. He was sprawled in a very nice stuffed chair. One Rosario had 'liberated' from a suite several cruises ago. Furniture got replaced all the time so Rosario had listed this chair as 'Damaged – seat torn'. It matched other items in the cabin, tiny as it was, that had formerly graced some of the better cabins on the ship.

"Yeah, you bring him the jewels and he gives you the money. And then you give me my share," Rosario said.

"Sure," J.J. said in that smooth voice that gained him access to so many places and so many women.

"Just don't forget we're partners when you get your hands on that money."

"Relax, there's gonna be plenty for both of us."

J.J. pulled a small green plastic frog from his pocket. He turned it over and over with his fingers as he considered the possibility that maybe he could avoid giving Rosario any of the money they would soon collect.

Rosario watched J.J. and wondered what he was thinking. As he wondered about J.J., Rosario's fingers traced over the bulge of the switchblade in his front pocket.

"All right," Rosario said, "then you fly Maui an' I hop off the ship when we get there an' meet you. We split the money an' life's beautiful. But I gotta get back on the ship an' finish the cruise, otherwise somebody might get suspicious."

"Wouldn't want that," J.J. said.

Rosario's eyes narrowed as he gave J.J. a hard look.

"You know this is serious business, right? You know I'm risking everything on this, right? You know we can't have any slip-ups, right?"

J.J. slid the small green plastic frog back into his pocket. In its place he pulled out a gold-chased cigarette case. He started to open the case.

"Hey, no smoking in my cabin," Rosario barked. "Smoking's not allowed in any cabin an' I don't want someone smelling smoke an' coming in my cabin to find something that I really don't want them to know about."

"Okay, okay, look," said J.J. "I'm putting it away. See, I'll wait until I can get up on deck to have a cigarette."

J.J. slid the fancy case back into his jacket pocket.

Rosario shook his head in disgust.

"All right," he said, "we do this thing the night before we get to Hilo. Let's go over it again, make sure we know exactly what we're doing."

J.J. wished he could slip out for a cigarette first, but agreed and soon they were reviewing their planned actions.

27

The women, with Koakane, had gathered in the main dining room for their Monday morning breakfast. They sat along the windows looking out at Honolulu. The ship had docked earlier that morning. They all had coffee and juice and they had all just returned heavily laden with plates from the breakfast buffet.

Looking out the window Teri saw Aloha Tower and noted the time on the clock at the top. Just after nine a.m. Craning her neck slightly she looked down and saw streams of passengers coming off the ship onto the dock. They headed away for a large opening in the building opposite the ship. It looked like a large warehouse and when she asked a waiter about it she was told that after disembarking and going through that building most everyone caught a tour bus or a taxi for the day's sightseeing.

The small group turned their attention to their plates and didn't talk much for the next ten minutes or so.

ဆဏ

"Well," said Haunani with her initial hunger satisfied, "what's everyone's plans for the day?" She took a bite of sourdough toast smeared with butter and guava jam. Followed that with a sip of coffee and looked at each of the others.

"Lori an' I are going shopping at Ala Moana Center," said Shari.

"Of course you are, girls," Haunani replied.

"Koakane and I have been talking about going to the Bishop Museum. I can barely remember the last time I was there and Koakane has never been there. Why don't you come with us, mom?" Teri said.

Haunani thought for moment and nodded her head.

"That would be nice. I haven't been there for a long time and there's a lot of our history there that I would like to see again. Thank you for the invitation. If you're sure I wouldn't be a third wheel, I'd love to join you."

"No problem," said Koakane, "besides, we're looking for someone to pick up the cab fare."

Haunani wrinkled her face up and stuck her tongue out at Koakane. Her reaction caused all of her daughters to laugh and Koakane to jump back in his chair.

Haunani picked up her fork and returned to her plate. But before putting some more of her scrambled eggs and sausage in her mouth she spoke again.

"Just remember, we have our last show to put on tonight. I want us to rehearse at four o'clock. Then dinner and a short rest before our eight o'clock show. Al our shows since we left San Francisco have been really well-received. I'd like this last show to be one everyone there will remember."

Haunani didn't realize just how much their audience would remember this last show of theirs.

After finishing breakfast, they all returned to their cabins to get ready, and then made their way down to the ship's deck where their identification cards were scanned into the ship's computer before disembarking. They then walked through the large warehouse-style building and out onto the street. Crossing the street to a taxi stand they got into two cabs, one to take Lori and Shari to Ala Moana Shopping Center, and one to take Teri, Haunani and Koakane to the Bishop Museum.

28

"Here you go, brother. Keep the change."

"Mahalo, enjoy the museum," the cab driver replied as he pulled out of the parking lot at the Bishop Museum.

Koakane turned and walked up the path, soon catching up with Haunani and Teri. Together the three of them made their way to the ticket booth and from there into the museum itself.

It was dark inside compared to the bright sunny day outside, but the exhibits were lighted well enough that they could make out all the details of the various items. They strolled through the museum, looking at displays of basketry, weapons, canoe paddles, tiki gods, ceremonial capes and replica models of canoes from throughout Polynesia. Overhead a shark, a whale skeleton and a turtle skeleton kept watch over them. Haunani pointed out exhibit items that related back to her ancestors.

They climbed the stairs, admiring the woodwork of those stairs and the railings that enclosed them. On the second floor they admired clothing from years gone by and photographs of Hawaiian royalty taken long ago.

Stopping in front of a large display case Haunani almost pressed her face to the glass while trying to get an even closer look at the items inside the case.

"Careful, Auntie, get too close an' maybe we have to include you in that display."

Teri's eyes grew wide as she imagined her mother's response. All three of them turned to find a large, quite large in fact, Security guard standing behind them . . .. with a grin on his face that lit up the whole area.

The hat on his head struggled, and failed, to contain a giant growth of curly reddish brown hair.

Haunani frowned at him, a line of wrinkles like incoming surf forming across her forehead.

Quick as a mongoose, she hit the guard on his shoulder with her purse.

"You damn boy, how you sneak up on your Auntie like that?"

"Owww," the guard yelped as he massaged his arm when Haunani's purse had struck. "Dang, you sure still feisty, Auntie Haunani."

Haunani gathered the guard into her arms and, in return, he wrapped his arms around her and lifted her off the floor.

"Buffalo! Put me down," she cried.

Teri and Koakane stood there, their mouths open.

Buffalo put Haunani down and watched, smiling, as she patted her hair back into place. She turned to Teri.

"Teri, this is my cousin Ava's son, Buffalo," she gave Buffalo a light whack on the arm. "Clumsy as a buffalo, this one . . . but sweet."

Buffalo hung his head in an *'Aw shucks'* stance.

"How's your mother?"

"Oh, good Auntie. She still works at the store every day."

Haunani turned to Teri and Koakane.

"Their family owns a little market out Kaneohe. Ava's husband died, oh, ten years or more ago."

"Thirteen," said Buffalo.

"How come my sisters and I don't know all this?" Teri said.

Haunani gazed fondly at Buffalo.

"They're here. We're on the Big Island. I never really leave there."

But then Buffalo had to ask how come his Auntie was over here in Honolulu, and then Haunani, with help from Teri, explained about the trip to Las Vegas, and the offer of free passage home for working on the ship. It took some time to catch up on things.

"No," Haunani was saying, "we don't have time to go out to Kaneohe. In fact," she looked at her watch, "we have to head back to the ship soon in order to rehearse for tonight's last performance."

"Well, really nice to see you Auntie. My mom gonna be sorry she missed you.

"Tell her come over to the Big Island sometime. An' bring you, if they can find a plane big enough."

Turning back to the display case behind them, Haunani looked once more. The case held, among other items, over twenty lei niho palaoa, carved whale tooth pendants suspended from human hair.

"There is so much mana here," Haunani said. She looked wistfully at one particular lei niho palaoa, one that hung in front of a drawing of Queen Ka'ahumanu. "It's too bad that lei niho of the Queen is separated from her. Oh, well, at least here it's safe."

After goodbyes, and hugs, Buffalo continued on his rounds. Haunani, Teri and Koakane finished their tour of the museum and headed back out to Bernice Street to flag down a cab to take them back to the ship.

ℬℭ

There were over thirty stores at the Ala Moana Center that specialized in women's fashion. Shari and Lori had touched base at each of them and as proof they carried nine shopping bags with them now. Eight of the bags were large . . . one was small but loudly emblazoned with the name of the store it came from . . . *Victoria's Secret.*

That bag was held by Shari . . . and looked askance at somewhat by Lori.

"You sure Teri won't get upset about those?"

"Nah, once she sees how much Koakane likes them, she'll really thank us."

"I don't know about that."

"Trust me," Shari said, "I know what men like."

You should, you've had enough of them, Lori thought.

"Okay," Lori said, "but we better get going. Mom will be upset if we're late for rehearsal."

The two women started for the exit.

"Oh, look," Shari said, "a Godiva chocolates store."

Lori knew they were going to be late for rehearsal . . . but, after all, they *were* Godiva chocolates.

29

Three rather large local men got off the flight from Kona to Honolulu. Each carried a large plastic flight bag such as could be bought in quantity at Costco.

While the men got off the plane separately, they grouped together down at the curb outside the interisland terminal. Hopping on a shuttle bus, they made their way over to the rental car area. They first asked about renting a compact car, but when the rental agent looked them up and down they switched their request to a full-size car.

"After all, we pretty full-size guys, yeah?" said Palani.

Palani paid cash for the car rental and for identification showed a Maui driver's license with the name Cheehula Kekealoha. The picture on the license barely resembled Palani, which did not matter much since the rental agent didn't bother looking at the photo.

ഇരു

Palani pulled into a parking space in the Zippy's lot. He, Vincent and Greyson walked in and squeezed into a booth.

"Okay, got plenty time," Palani said, "so let's eat."

The waitress was soon kept busy bringing plates loaded with chili and spaghetti, oxtail soup and fried chicken, cheeseburgers and macaroni salad to the men's table. But Greyson told the waitress to cancel Vincent's order of Portuguese bean soup.

"You can't open the windows on the car enough to air it out after you eat that soup," Greyson told Vincent. "An' I'm sitting in the back behind you. I like breathe on our way to the museum."

Vincent pouted a little, but made up for it by ordering another Teriyaki Prime Burger for himself, along with an order of fries.

The men took their time eating and reviewed, very quietly, their plans for the evening. When the sun went down outside they got up, visited the bathroom, and left a very generous tip for the waitress. She felt it was only right considering how much time she'd had to spend on their table.

30

"Okay, that's pretty good," said Haunani from where she sat on the stage floor. She held a tall double gourd, an ipu heke, with her right hand and struck it with her left when she was giving the group their rhythm. "But Lori, you're just about a half beat behind the other girls. Try and catch up. This is our last performance tonight. We want to look good."

"No problem, Mom," said Shari as she pushed her chest out. "I'll look good no matter what."

Shari swiveled her head to glance at Koakane.

"Maybe you should oil up those muscles a little more for the show. All these old ladies are expecting a fine sight from you, while their old men are watching us wahine."

Teri huffed and, turning away, walked to the edge of the small stage.

Shari's eyes twinkled and she searched for something else to say to get Teri's goat.

Haunani slammed her ipu onto the stage.

"Shari, no more. Teri, no let her get under your skin. Koakane . . . maybe a little more oil for this last show wouldn't hurt."

Haunani used the ipu heke to brace on as she stood.

"Good thing I only gonna do two dances. I'm so stiff from being cooped up in this ship. Can't wait to get home now."

"Us too, Mom," said Teri as she came back to the middle of the group.

"All right, let's go through 'Lovely Hula Hands' one more time. Then we'll call it a day and go rest up before dinner. An' remember, no eat too much tonight before the show," Haunani said and looking straight at Shari, "when you bend during the dance I don't want you making fut tonight like last time."

Teri covered her mouth to keep from laughing out loud. Lori grinned widely while Shari's jaw dropped and she started to sputter.

"Yeah," said Koakane, "especially since you were right in front of me then."

"Places everyone," said Haunani, ignoring the sputtering noises still coming out of Shari's mouth.

31

The rental car with the three big men in it came down Bernice Street and parked just before the entrance to the museum grounds.

"Careful," Vincent said, "no block the driveway. We don' want the cops coming around and giving us a ticket."

"You worry too much," Palani said.

"You jus' be glad I worry. My worrying keeps us out of jail."

The three men looked out the windows of the car and, having made sure there was no one to see them, they each took a bandana from their large plastic carry-on bag. They put the bandanas around their necks, but didn't pull them up over their faces.

Across the museum grounds they could see lights and hear music and laughter. A giant white tent was set up and with the sides rolled up they could see people moving around buffet tables while servers distributed champagne and other drinks. A party was in progress, just as Buffalo had told them it would be. The Visitor Parking lot was close to full with cars.

The men walked across the grass, around to the right of the Café where they had eaten with Buffalo and made their way toward the Hawaiian Hall. As they neared the museum they glanced around to be sure they were unobserved, and then pulled their bandanas up over the lower portion of their faces.

"He's gonna turn off the cameras, right?" Greyson said.

"Yeah, that's the plan," said Vincent.

"Then why we need to wear bandanas?"

"You met him," said Vincent continuing on toward the museum, "You trust him to get it all right?"

Greyson nodded and pulled his bandana a little tighter, all the while thinking to himself . . . *I hope so, I sure hope so.*

32

"Hey, Larry," Buffalo called to the other night security guard.

"What?

"I gotta go make shi-shi."

"You wouldn't have to piss so much if you didn't drink so many of those thirty-two ouncers."

Buffalo shrugged.

"I gotta stay hydrated."

"You're not hydrated, you're water-logged. Hurry up, I think they gonna start dancing soon."

"Yeah, yeah. I be right back," said Buffalo as he left the area in front of the Science Adventure Center where the fancy party was taking place, and headed uphill toward the Hawaiian Hall.

Once at the Hall he unlocked the front door, stepped inside and made his way to a koa panel set into the wall. Looking around he shivered at the shadows deeper inside the museum. Buffalo turned back to the koa panel, unlocked it with another key and flipped all the switches inside to "Off". With the alarms as well as the closed circuit video cameras turned off Buffalo looked once more at the dark shadows inside. He backed up to the door and stepped outside, barely avoiding a collision with the first of three dark figures entering the building.

"Here," he said as he dropped three keys into the outstretched hand of the man.

"Mahalo," said Vincent.

"Jus' don' take too long. My partner probably gonna wanna use da bathroom soon too."

33

Buffalo closed the door behind him and headed back across the lawn toward the Science Center and the party tent.

Inside the Hawaiian Hall the three men moved rapidly up to the second floor where the majority of the lei niho were displayed. Once on the second floor Vincent gave Greyson and Palani each a display case key along with a small flashlight from his carry-on bag. They spread out.

Though the museum was dark and filled with shadows, it wasn't totally black. There was still a good deal of light filtering down from the giant skylight at the top of the building. That light, and the light from their flashlights, made their work easy.

Spreading out on the second floor they each attacked a different group of display cases. The copied keys allowed them access and once they had a display case opened it was just a matter of reaching in and taking out the lei niho inside. Their carry-on bags filled quickly. Within about twenty minutes each of them had 40 to 50 lei niho in his bag. The men made their way up to the third floor and collected a few more lei niho each from two display cases there.

Vincent opened one final display case. Pictures inside depicted a warrior chief from the very early history of the islands. An old club, nicked and cracked from use in battle, hung from hooks on the back wall of the display case. A yellowed lei niho made from a sperm whale tooth hung beside the warclub, suspended by a rope of human hair. The floor of the display case had other stuff, like several kukui nuts and a palm branch, to make everything look authentic. The card explaining this exhibit stated that not only was the lei niho that of the chief, but the hair that it hung by was his own too. Vincent reached in and grasped the lei niho. He pulled, but the ancient lei niho would not come loose from the hook it hung off. Try as he might Vincent could not work the lei niho loose.

"Hey, listen old man," Vincent said, "I not try steal your necklace. I just gonna put 'em back in the ground, so your mana can go back into the islands where it belongs."

The lei niho still refused to budge.

"Please," Vincent said, "I respect you and all the Ali'i from the past. Please let me do this out of the respect that I have for you."

Frustrated, Vincent let go of the lei niho and began to back up. He stopped when the lei niho slipped off the hook and fell with a plop to the bottom of the display case. It rested on a picture of the chief, with the lei niho around his neck.

Vincent picked up the lei niho palaoa, held it in his palm and bowed his head. He took a step backwards, turned and placed the antique item in his bag, gently. Turning, he began to walk away and only then did he think to himself *Shit, probably got caught on the hook just a little, and when I pulled it loosened, and then when I let go it just fell by itself. Nothing else.*

A little further down the corridor something hit him in the back of his head.

"Oww," he said as he reached up to rub the spot.

Looking down, Vincent saw a kukui nut on the floor. Looking back, he saw the door to the display case slowly swing closed. He heard the latch engage.

He walked much more quickly to join the others.

The men came together at the head of the staircase.

"Okay? We got enough?" Palani said.

"Yeah," said Vincent, "looks good. Give me your keys and I'll toss them after we drive away."

"I'll be glad to be out of here," said Palani. "Place gives me the creeps."

"You scare?" Vincent said.

"Nah, jus' . . .. I jus' feel like I'm being watched."

"Well, I told you . . . there's lot of mana in this place. Which is why," Vincent raised his voice as he looked around and tried to see what might be in the shadows, "that's why we're returning these lei niho to the aina. To make the land better, to bring the power back again."

Silence descended upon the three men.

Palani shivered.

"Let's go," said Greyson, and the three men clattered down the stairs and out the front doors of the Hawaiian Hall. Keeping to the shadows of the trees and buildings, they made their way back to their car.

They pulled away from the curb and set out for the airport and the last flights of the evening.

As they merged onto the freeway, Vincent dropped the three display case keys out the window of the rental car.

34

"All right, let's get moving, wiki wiki everyone," Haunani stood in her suite with a large woven basket containing items she had decided they just might need for the evenings' show.

A chorus of "Okay, Mom," greeted her words.

Except from Shari.

"C'mon, Mom, it's just another show for all these touristas."

Haunani turned toward Shari.

"It's the last show. Maybe the last show we'll ever do on this boat."

"Ship."

Haunani turned toward Koakane, sitting on the sofa with Teri sitting on the arm of the sofa next to him.

"What?" said Haunani.

"It's a ship, not a boat," said Koakane.

"What's the difference?" said Shari.

"A boat doesn't travel across the ocean, a ship does."

"Whatever."

"Well then," said Haunani, "let's go up to the lounge and make this last show . . . on this ship . . . our best one yet. I want us to make it truly memorable for everyone who comes to watch us."

And with that directive, Haunani led her small troupe out of the suite and up to the cocktail lounge two decks up.

It was to be a truly memorable show.

35

Up on the top cabin deck, in her suite, Marilyn Hardin entertained the Captain, the First Mate and the Recreation Director.

Two empty champagne glasses sat on the glass-topped table in front of the couch. An ice bucket with an upturned champagne bottle left a ring of condensation on the table. Several discarded napkins lay strewn about on the table top.

The Captain twirled his glass by the stem watching the bubbles twist and turn. Through the wide glass doors of the suite he could see little beyond the balcony outside. But he could feel the motion of his ship as they plowed through the water on their run toward Hilo. Only a half hour before he had given final orders up on the Bridge after guiding his ship out of Honolulu where it had been docked by the old Clock Tower. The others had arrived down in Marilyn's suite before him, but they all, excluding Marilyn, rose when he entered the cabin after a perfunctory knock on the door.

The Captain set his glass down on the cocktail table, not bothering with the last sip left in the glass.

Sitting at one end of the couch, Marilyn tipped her head back to catch the last few drops of champagne from her glass before putting it beside the others on the table.

"Oh, I do love drinking bubbly water. And that was some of the best I've had."

It should do, thought the Captain as he glanced at the upside down bottle. The white flowers painted on its front along with the name, Pierre-Jouét, proclaimed its quality . . . and price.

"Well," said the Captain, "we should be going Ms. Hardin. The show has probably already started."

"Yes, these women have been very punctual in performing," the Recreation Director said.

"But I'm so tired," Marilyn said leaning back on the couch as she crossed her legs. An impressive display of tanned thigh greeted the three men.

The Captain glanced up at the ceiling and then looked back at Marilyn's face. He noted the slight smirk she wore.

"I understand," he said, "but we did promise the other passengers that you would attend tonight's show." He held in reserve a comment about the hundred thousand dollars she had been paid, in addition to her free passage, for her appearance on the ship.

"And we have reserved a table for you," said the Recreation Director.

"With more champagne?" Marilyn asked.

"Of course," said the Captain.

"Well, in that case . . . we may as well go."

Marilyn extended her hand to the First Mate who rose, lightly gripped her fingers and assisted her to her feet. He was rewarded for his gallantry with a brief look down her top. To his credit, he did not blush when he saw that she was braless . . . again.

36

As Marilyn, along with the three ship's officers, exited her suite she paid no attention to the cabin steward using a white cloth to wipe an imaginary stain off the corridor wall. The three men were too focused on Ms. Hardin and too used to seeing Rosario to pay him any attention.

Rosario watched the four of them walk away down the corridor and turn in to the elevator lobby. He waited until he heard the sound of their footsteps entering an elevator. He waited a few moments longer and then made his way to the elevator lobby himself. Picking up a white house phone from where it hung in the corner beside the elevators Rosario dialed an extension. As he waited for the phone to be answered, he watched the floor numbers for the elevators. The one closest to him had stopped one floor above. Rosario imagined the four occupants getting out of the elevator and heading toward the cocktail lounge where the hula group was performing.

His thoughts were interrupted as someone picked up the phone at the other end.

"Yeah?"

"Time to get started."

"On my way."

Rosario hung up the house phone and gave it a quick wipe down with the cloth in his hand. He rocked back and forth waiting.

The middle elevator stopped on Rosario's floor and the doors opened to allow J.J. to exit. Immediately Rosario turned, stepped from the elevator lobby to the corridor and walked up toward Ms. Hardin's suite. J.J. followed one step behind Rosario.

37

Palani and Greyson raced for the check-in counter at Honolulu International, showed their identification and then raced again over to the security checkpoint. Their bags went through x-ray without having to be opened and, since they had planned carefully, the few metal objects they had on them fit nicely into small round dishes and also passed through the x-ray machine.

Collecting their belongings, they again ran for their gates, Palani headed for a flight to Maui while Greyson ran to catch a flight to Kona.

They each made their plane, but Greyson only made it by flashing a charming smile at the good-looking ticket agent at the gate. The agent looked Greyson up and down and smiled back as he led Greyson down the ramp to the plane.

ᏉᏣ

Once in the air, with their carry-on bags stowed in the overhead bin, each man relaxed.

Palani, on his Maui flight, ordered a beer.

Greyson waved the flight attendant away and looked out the window as the plane banked for Kona. Below he saw a large brightly lit cruise liner, making its way along the same path he was taking.

"Lucky buggahs," he mouthed under his breath. "Nothing to do but eat an' drink an' relax. No worries. No pilikia . . . no pilikia to disturb they trip."

Greyson leaned back and tried to relax. It was difficult knowing the task that lay ahead of him.

38

Rosario and J.J. walked confidently up the corridor and stopped in front of Marilyn Hardin's suite. JJ carried a small empty aluminum briefcase. Rosario carried three clean white towels, looking as if he had been called upon to replace some linens. When the two men paused in front of the door, Rosario looked casually up and down the corridor. He then produced his master key card and unlocked the door.

"Housekeeping, Ms. Hardin," he called to the empty cabin.

Rosario stepped inside, holding the door open behind him. J.J. stayed out of sight around the corner of the door.

"Ms. Hardin, Housekeeping" Rosario called again. When he received on response he motioned to J.J. to follow him into the room. They closed the door behind them. Rosario did not bother to double-bolt the door, after all, Marilyn Hardin would be at that hula for a long time.

"Okay, J.J., the safe is inside the bedroom closet."

"I know that. Just let me get to work."

The two men stepped into the suite's bedroom, Rosario shaking his head at the mess Marilyn had left. Clothes tossed on the bed and draped over chairs. Open bottles of makeup left on the nightstand.

J.J. focused on his task, pulled on a pair of latex gloves and opened the closet door. On a shelf at eye-level sat the in-room safe.   From an inside jacket pocket J.J. withdrew a small mechanic's stethoscope. Fixing its molded rubber earpieces into his ears he placed the resonator at the other end against the door of the safe. He pulled on the handle to check that Marilyn hadn't just left the safe open. Foiled there, J.J. concentrated on listening as he began turning the dial.

39

Haunani and her troupe were almost halfway through their itinerary when Marilyn, accompanied by the three ship's officers, entered the cocktail lounge. Following Marilyn, the four of them made their way between the tables to a table with a *Reserved* sign on it that sat just in front of the stage. The little group ignored the fact that the hula troupe was in the middle of a number.

The Captain signaled a waiter who took their orders and quickly ducked out to have them filled.

Marilyn Hardin leaned back in her chair and looked around the room, flashing her famous movie smile at everyone in the room. Cameras began recording her presence as her smile broadened.

The waiter returned with champagne cocktails for everyone at Marilyn's table.

৪৩জ্ঞ

The women brought their dance to a close to distracted applause.

"All right," Haunani said into the microphone placed on the front of the stage, "gentlemen . . . and ladies," Haunani flashed a smile toward Marilyn's table, a smile dripping with venom, "it's time for the dance that made Hawaii such a favorite wedding destination . . . 'Ke Kali Nei Au' more popularly known as the

Hawaiian Wedding Song. Please welcome my daughter, Iwalani, and our handsome kane, Koakane."

For the shows they had been performing, Haunani had taken to referring to her daughters by their Hawaiian middle names.

Teri came from behind the curtain set up at the back of the stage, now wearing a long white gown. She turned to her right. Koakane also came from behind the curtain and turned to his left. Koakane was wearing a white malo around his waist and a haku lei around his head.

Both performers smiled with thousand watt brilliance. The women in the audience eventually looked up at Koakane's smile, dreams of romantic bliss filling their eyes.

Teri and Koakane had been behind the curtain, awaiting their cue, when Marilyn and her group entered the lounge. They both extended an arm in greeting to the audience and swept their arms across the audience, their intention being to end with their hands extended to each other.

Teri completed her greeting. Koakane did not. His movement ceased halfway when he caught a glimpse of Marilyn Hardin at her table with the ship's officers. His outstretched hand pointed toward Marilyn's table.

Marilyn smiled up at Koakane, thinking that he was acknowledging her. He wasn't.

"You! You bitch. How can you sit there and smile and drink champagne when you caused so many men to die in

Vietnam. And because of you, others were beaten to within an inch of their lives. My uncle was one of those men. He was beaten for ten days straight after you gave the prison camp commandant the secret message that he trusted you with. He thought you would let his family, and the world, know that he was alive and being kept in a prison camp in Vietnam. Instead you gave his message, written on a scrap of his uniform, to the commandant. My uncle was strung up in his cell and beaten with bamboo rods every day for ten days. They only stopped beating him when another prisoner died from the same sort of beating."

Koakane dropped his arm and stepped forward to the edge of the stage.

"And you walked out of that camp and left those American prisoners behind. You went back to the glitz of Hollywood and went on talk shows and told everyone how awful we were to the North Vietnamese. You never talked about the men you left behind you in that prison camp. You should have been hung! You should have been executed as a traitor to the United States. I'd carry out that execution today if I could."

Koakane took a step back.

"I'm not going to entertain you. I despise you and hope you burn in hell someday. Traitorous bitch."

Koakane turned and walked toward the back curtain of the stage.

Haunani looked as if she was going to say something to him, but remained silent.

Teri looked at her mother and then followed Koakane through the curtain to the back dressing area.

The audience sat in shocked silence . . . all except for one grizzled vet at the back of the room he nodded his head in agreement and lightly applauded Koakane's words.

40

Marilyn sat, with her mouth open, as Koakane, followed by Teri, exited through the back curtain on the stage. She looked around the room and saw the stunned audience . . . though quite a few of them had cell phones out and were recording the event.

Standing up, Marilyn glared at the three ships officers who shared her table.

"You," she barked, looking directly at the Captain, "aren't you going to do anything? Are you just going to let him speak to me like that? Aren't you going to, oh, I don't know, clap him in irons?" She didn't bother to lower her voice.

The Captain took a sip from his champagne glass, held it up by the stem and looked at the tiny bubbles slowly rising inside the glass.

Quietly the Captain replied to her tirade.

"I'm afraid we don't do clapping in irons anymore, Ms. Hardin. But I assure you I will have a meeting with him and I can also assure you that this group will never perform again on my ship."

The Captain put his glass back on the table and stared up at the furious Marilyn Hardin.

"That's it? A meeting with him? Slap his wrist and say don't do that ever again? That's all?"

The Captain continued to stare at Marilyn . . . noticing how the veins in her face stood out, how flushed her face had become, and also, perhaps for the first time, how wrinkled and crepe-like the skin around her neck was.

"The entire group will be put off the ship in Hilo," he said, knowing full well that that had been the schedule all the time. "We will replace them with another group, perhaps more to your liking."

"That is not good enough," Marilyn spit out the words. "I want you to do more."

"What should I do?"

"I want a full and complete apology from him, and from every member of their group."

"Small chance that," Shari said in a stage whisper that Marilyn easily heard.

Marilyn spun, glared at the troupe, and then turned back to the Captain and his men.

"I shall be in my cabin. And I expect that apology before we arrive at our next port."

"Hilo," the Captain supplied.

"Hilo. Or I shall leave the ship there . . . and exert all my energy in seeing that you are removed from your position, and that no one else ever sets sail on this ship."

Marilyn picked up her champagne glass, gulped half of it down and dropped the glass in the center of the table where the rest of her champagne ran across the table and dripped off and onto the First Mate's lap.

"I'm leaving now," she said, and she made her way back through the lounge and out the doors.

The room was silent for a moment.

Haunani stepped to the front of the stage.

"We have one more dance, would you all like to see us perform it?"

The audience responded enthusiastically.

One man in the back, with a few too many mai tais under his belt, called out, "This is the best show I've seen all week."

Haunani addressed her daughters, settling them into position. Teri came through the curtain in a new outfit to join them, and the group moved into the farewell dance that they had rehearsed that afternoon.

As the final dance went on, Haunani thought to herself, *Well, we never meant to make a career out of performing on this ship.*

41

JJ had the safe open. He removed the many little jewelry bags and spread them on the bed. Together he and Rosario opened and viewed the contents of each bag.

"Now that's a haul," JJ said.

JJ set the small aluminum briefcase on the bed and opened it. One by one he placed the many jewelry bags inside. As he slipped the last jewelry bag in JJ pulled the little green frog from his jacket pocket and dropped it in one of the jewelry bags.

"I've had good luck ever since I picked that up in Vegas," he said when Rosario looked at him with questioning eyes.

"Whatever," Rosario said, "Let's get out of here."

JJ closed the briefcase before closing and locking the safe door. They stepped out of the bedroom area of the suite and into the living room. Both men looked carefully around the suite to be sure there was nothing left out to connect them to the robbery. They moved toward the door.

Just then the handle turned and the door to the suite opened.

42

Marilyn froze in place, but her years of being a celebrity, of being noticed and fawned over and of always having her way kicked in. It never crossed her mind that anyone would do anything but what she wanted them to do.

"What are you doing in my room?"

And then she made her fatal mistake.

Marilyn stepped into the cabin and let the door close behind her. She took a step forward and looked at the small aluminum briefcase in JJ's hand.

"What is that? What do you have in that case?"

Marilyn swept past the two men into her bedroom. She spun the combination on the safe and wrenched the door open. One look inside brought her back out into the living room portion of the luxurious suite.

"Where are my jewels?"

The high pitch of her voice hurt JJ's ears.

Marilyn's eyes focused on the small aluminum briefcase again.

"What do you have in there?" she demanded pointing at the briefcase. "Give me that," she said extending her hand.

The two men looked at each other. Never having been in this type of situation before, JJ handed over the briefcase.

Marilyn stepped over to the couch, placed the briefcase down on it and opened the case. She took out one of the velvet pouches, pulled it open and poured the pearl necklace inside the pouch into her hand.

"You were stealing my jewels," she said looking up at JJ who stood in front of her. She paid no attention to the meek-looking room steward who stood behind her.

"Such famous last words," said Rosario as he grabbed the empty champagne bottle and smashed it down onto the back of Marilyn Hardin's head. The bottle was harder than her head. It held together, while her skull caved in.

43

"Oh, shit man, what did you do?" JJ said.

"It's okay. She would have been able to identify us. And now she can't."

"Man, I did not agree to murder. Robbery, but not murder."

"Tough. We're in this together."

"But you're the one who hit her."

"Look, talk later. Right now we have to get out of here before anyone comes along."

"Shall we dump her over the railing?" asked J.J.

"No, ship's got cameras watching the decks. They might pick up her body going in the water. Besides, we'll have more time to sort things out if we just leave her here. No one will find her for a long time. Let's clean up and get out of here."

Rosario wiped the neck of the bottle with a discarded napkin, then placed the bottle beside Marilyn's lifeless body. He picked up the pearls, slipped them back into their velvet sack and returned the sack to the briefcase.

"Here," he said thrusting the open briefcase into JJ's hands. "Did we touch anything else?"

JJ shook his head, his eyes still focused on the woman's body, and on the bloody circle around her head.

"Okay then, let's go," Rosario said. He used another napkin to grip the doorknob with as he opened the door. Stepping out he looked up and down the corridor before signaling JJ to join him.

While Rosario's attention was focused outside on the corridor, J.J. took two of the smaller velvet bags out of the briefcase and dropped them into the side pocket of his jacket.

"Give me the door card." When JJ just stood there Rosario added, "Inside. In the little pocket."

JJ turned and picked the card from its pocket on the inside of the door and handed it to Rosario.

Rosario tossed the napkin into the room and pulled the door shut with the edge of his hand, being careful not to leave his fingerprints behind.

"Put the card in the slot, 'Do Not Disturb' side up," Rosario said. "That way no one will find her for a long time. Let's go."

JJ slipped the card into the slot on the door handle. 'Do Not Disturb' side up. Rosario didn't bother telling JJ to wipe his fingerprints off the room card.

"Make sure the door closed," Rosario said as he started walking down the corridor.

JJ dutifully hit the door with his shoulder. It was closed and locked.

As he hurried to catch up with Rosario, JJ failed to notice that his shaking the door had caused the room card to fall out. It landed on the floor in front of the doorway with the side facing up reading '*Room Service Please*'.

44

It was a somber group of entertainers who gathered in Haunani's cabin. Shari poured drinks for everyone in an attempt to lighten up the mood of the group. Teri sat on the very end of the couch, her arms folded across her chest, trying to decide who to be mad at . . . Koakane or that woman that he had yelled at. Lori evidently found some humor in the situation because she stood by the sliding glass doors leading to the balcony with a tight grin on her face and the glass of wine from Shari in her hand. She took frequent sips.

Haunani sat in one of the chairs thinking back through the evening's events. Now and then she glanced over at Koakane, standing with his back to the cabin door and looking down at his feet.

"Well," said Haunani. "That was certainly a new experience for us. Having our dancing interrupted. And then getting a dressing-down from the Captain himself. But then, I don't suppose we ever really wanted to perform on this ship again, did we? And I think my only real concern is whether or not this will affect the guests at our weekly luau back at our home."

"Oh, I don't think we have to worry about that," Lori said. "The guests at my hotel are always looking for something to liven things up. If they do hear about this 'incident' it will probably just make them curious to see the 'wild man' who caused all the commotion."

"That's not fair," Teri said. "You heard what Koakane said about that woman. She did terrible things during the Vietnam war . . . and she got away with them. Someone had to call her out."

"But maybe at some better time, eh?" Shari said.

"Sorry," said Koakane, looking up at all the women. "I lost it. I've been boiling inside ever since I first saw that poster about her being on the trip. A lotta vets I know would like to crack her one across the mouth."

"Would you hit a woman? Even that woman?" asked Teri.

Koakane thought for a moment.

"No . . . not even here. I just wouldn't be able to do it."

"Good," said Teri, "that's nice to know."

Koakane stood up straighter. A puzzled look came over his face, but he said nothing further.

45

Deep in the bowels of the ship, Rosario opened his cabin door, stepped inside and motioned to J.J. to get himself inside too. Rosario closed the door behind J.J. and put on the privacy lock. J.J. set the briefcase down on the couch.

"What a cockup," J.J. said.

"Don't worry," Rosario said, "we're clean. Made sure we left no prints. You get off tomorrow with the jewels, contact our buyer, get the money from him, fly to Maui and I meet you there. We split 50-50 and life is beautiful. You go wherever you want – I come back to the ship, finish the cruise and then turn in my notice. Lots of people quit after a cruise so there's always new people coming on. Nothing unusual there."

J.J. turned to the briefcase on the couch and gave it a tap with his finger.

"Lotta money in here," he said.

Rosario remained silent.

"And now I gotta take all the risk getting it off the ship . . . selling these jewels for less than they're worth . . . and then risk flying to Maui just to give you half. If not for that I could fly straight out of Kona and be out of sight the same day."

J.J. had said too much . . . but he didn't realize it.

"You know, I'm taking a lot more of the risk than you," J.J. continued, "I should get a bigger slice of the take."

"You think so?" said Rosario.

"Yeah, I do. I think I should get seventy-five percent."

"And I only get twenty-five percent?

J.J. furrowed his brow in thought.

"Well, you set this all up. And you killed that woman. So . . maybe you should get thirty-five percent."

"Generous of you," said Rosario.

"I think so. Plus, I need a little extra so that if the cops ever question me, I don't know anything about how she got hit on the head . . . or by who."

It was Rosario's turn to think.

"Okay," he finally said, "sixty-five and thirty-five. Shake," Rosario said extending his left hand.

It was a little awkward, but J.J. gripped Rosario's hand.

Rosario clasped J.J.'s hand, tightly. Then he shoved J.J.'s hand up and at the same time brought his switchblade out of his pocket, snapped it open and plunged it into J.J.'s chest, just below his sternum.

Rosario angled the blade upwards and jerked it from side to side slicing through J.J.'s heart several times. Only a little blood leaked out around the wound. J.J.'s eyes went wide. He tried to speak, failed and fell back onto the floor of the cabin, the knife still stuck in his chest. He was already dead as he struck the floor.

Rosario stood looking down at the body. He began turning over in his mind what his next moves should be. Without J.J. he needed to find another way to get the stolen jewelry off the ship. The answer popped into his head. Grabbing the briefcase, he stepped over to his cabin door, opened it and peered outside. The corridor was empty. He took a moment to step back in, pull the pillowcase off his bed pillow, removed the jewelry pouches from the briefcase and dump them into the pillowcase. Leaving the aluminum briefcase on his bed he stepped out into the corridor, pulled the door shut behind him and placed the "Do Not Disturb" card into the keycard slot. He tucked the pillowcase under his arm.

Rosario headed up the corridor toward the elevators. Once inside he pushed the button for one of the top floors. As he traveled upwards his eyes looked over the ceiling of the elevator. A grin spread slowly across his face.

46

When he reached the floor where Haunani and her girls had cabins, Rosario slowed and walked up to the door of the cabin that Teri and Shari shared. He took out his master key and inserted it in the slot. He was pleased to notice that there was no "Do Not Disturb" card in the key slot.

"Housekeeping," he called as he opened the door.

Empty.

Rosario closed the door behind him, flipped the dead bolt shut and moved quickly across the room. In the corner, just where he had remembered putting them, were the two shopping bags filled with packages of beef jerky from Las Vegas. Squatting down Rosario emptied the two bags onto the carpet. He dumped the velvet jewelry bags out of the pillowcase and proceeded to place half of the jewelry bags at the bottom of each shopping bag. Once that was accomplished he filled each bag with the packages of jerky. He lifted each and found that they were not appreciably heavier than when they had held only jerky packages.

As he stood up a thought crossed his mind. He stepped into the bedroom section of the cabin and professionally turned down the covers. He was slightly irritated that he had no chocolates to put on the pillows, but decided they'd have to do without tonight.

Folding the empty pillowcase and tucking it under his arm, Rosario walked back to the cabin door, pulled it open and stepped outside.

Just as he was closing the door behind him the door to Haunani's cabin opened and Teri stepped out followed by Koakane.

Rosario gave a practiced thousand-watt smile and a slight nod of his head.

"Bed's all ready now. Last night on the ship, eh?"

Teri smiled back, but Koakane frowned slightly.

"Yes," Teri said, "we go home tomorrow."

"Good," said Rosario. "Have a safe trip home, but maybe come back again sometime. Good night."

Rosario turned and walked away before either Teri or Koakane had a chance to say anything further.

Teri turned to Koakane who shrugged and indicated his cabin door with a nod. Arm in arm they walked over to Koakane's cabin. He opened the door and stood aside as Teri stepped in. Koakane followed, pausing only long enough to place the "Do Not Disturb" card in the key slot of the door.

47

Back in his cabin, with the deadbolt set on the door behind him, Rosario thought deeply about his next moves. Stepping over to J.J.'s body, he removed all the items in J.J.'s pockets. He kept the money from J.J.'s wallet and put J.J.'s door keycard into his own pocket. He already had an idea how that card would come in handy. He pulled the knife from J.J.'s chest, cleaned it on the dead man's shirt, closed it and put it back in his pocket. He knew that at some point he would have to dispose of the knife, and that made him sad. He'd had that knife ever since he was sixteen years old.

There was no blood on the carpet or anywhere else in the cabin. His mind traveled back to the ship's elevators and he grinned again. He knew what to do now. It was just a matter of waiting for the right time.

Rosario stepped over the dead body and sat down on the couch. He picked up the tv remote laying on the couch and turned on the cabin's small-screen tv. Flipping through the channels he found a fairly current movie that he had yet to see. Well, now was the time. He settled back, checked his watch and relaxed.

48

Vincent had to pound on his sister's front door in order to wake her up from where she slept on the couch in front of the tv.

"Whaaat!" she demanded when she got the front door open.

"Hey, sis, I need to crash with you tonight."

Beatrice turned away from the open door and headed back to the couch.

"Go sleep with Billy," she said and plopped back onto the couch. "What's in the bag?" she asked.

"You don't want to know," Vincent said as he stepped in, closed the door behind him and made his way down the short hallway to his nephew's room.

What a mess, he thought as he opened the door and flicked on the light switch.

"Hey, what?" fifteen-year-old Billy said pushing himself up on one elbow and squinting into the light.

"Jus' me, your Uncle Vincent. Your mom say I gotta crash with you tonight. So move over."

Grumbling, Billy moved to one side of the bed.

"Okay, Unc, but no fart like you always do."

Vincent turned out the light, felt his way over to the bed and climbed in. Then, a big smile on his face, he let go with a humungous fart.

"Awww, shit," said Billy pulling the blanket tightly over his nose.

℘℧

Palani roused an auntie of his from her sleep over on Maui. Since she only had a tiny one-bedroom in Kahalui, he had to squeeze himself onto her couch in the living room. She was concerned about his bag, thinking maybe he planned to stay more than the one night, but decided not to ask about it. Maybe then he'd leave in the morning.

℘℧

Greyson used his cell phone to call a friend from the airport. Some twenty minutes later his friend picked him up outside the Kona terminal.

Greyson humped his bag into the back seat and climbed into the front passenger seat.

"Hello, Tommy," he said giving a quick peck on the cheek to his friend, a haole guy with blond hair, freckles and a perpetual sunburn.

"Yeah, yeah. How come I only hear from you when you need some favor?"

"Not true . . . is it? Tell you want, in appreciation of all you do for me, tonight you can ask any favor of me."

"Ohhhh," Tommy's eyes lit up and he sat up straighter in the driver's seat. "Any favor?"

"Any favor," Greyson said smiling, while thinking to himself, *God, you're so bland.*

Tommy pulled away from the terminal humming *I Can Do That* from *Chorus Line.*

49

At three a.m. Rosario roused himself from his couch. Stepping out into the corridor outside his cabin, after first checking that it was empty, he made his way to a laundry storage room. There he selected an empty rolling laundry cart which he brought back to his cabin. He knew this was the risky part. Since the cart would not fit though the door to his cabin, he left it outside, propped the door open and stepped back to the dead body.

J.J. was heavier than Rosario had thought, but with a great deal of effort, and a lot of cursing under his breath, he managed to haul the dead man over to the laundry cart and dump him in. Rosario retrieved several towels from his bathroom and arranged them over the dead body in the cart. Looking back into the room for one final check, he remembered the aluminum briefcase and stuffed it under the towels on top of J.J.'s body.

Closing the door to his cabin, Rosario pushed the cart down the corridor toward the elevators.

ℬ℧

Rosario took the elevator to the next to highest deck on the ship. With the laundry cart blocking his elevator door open, he pushed the button and brought the elevator next to his to the same deck.

Retrieving a keyring from his pocket, Rosario located a key that he had stolen from the elevator repairman several cruises ago. He'd known then that it would come in handy someday.

Using that master key, Rosario locked the second elevator in place on the lower deck. He returned to the first elevator, pulled the laundry cart inside and went up one more deck.

This was the top deck of the ship and Rosario again used his laundry cart to block the door open. Then, with a great deal of effort, he hauled J.J.'s body out of the cart and over to the closed doors of the second elevator.

Having carefully observed the elevator repairman one afternoon, he used the master key to get the elevator doors open. He looked down to the elevator itself, still locked in place one deck below.

Rosario pushed J.J.'s body into the elevator shaft and was pleased to see it land on the roof of the elevator below.

Again using the elevator master key, he closed the doors on the second elevator, took the first elevator down to the deck below and released the second elevator so that it could be used once more.

Then Rosario took the first elevator down to his floor, punched the button to take it back up to the ship's lobby level, and returned to his room. He lay down on his bed without taking off his clothes and thought briefly about his upcoming morning activities . . . and drifted off to sleep.

50

Without benefit of an alarm clock, Rosario awoke at six a.m. The ceased motion of the ship woke him and told him that they were now docked in Hilo.

Rosario set off for the employee cafeteria on the floor below his cabin. There he ate heartily. The other employees that he shared a table with commented on his appetite. *Nothing like a killing to give you an appetite*, Rosario thought smiling at his tablemates.

Finished with breakfast, Rosario returned to his cabin. He changed from his ship's uniform into his going-ashore clothes. Then he spent ten minutes packing an airline carry-on bag with those things he wanted to keep. Some items from his cabin went down the toilet. Others he bundled up and dropped in a trash bin on the floor below, just outside the employee cafeteria.

Back in his room Rosario checked carefully to be sure he'd left nothing that could incriminate him. His knife was tucked into his right front pocket and he touched it repeatedly.

Satisfied, Rosario took out his cellphone. He looked up a number from his Contacts list and called it.

"Hello, yes, I need to rent a car. Just for today. Yes, I'll return it here in Hilo. Yes, I'll be there to pick it up within the hour. Aloha."

Retrieving a business card from his wallet, Rosario made a second call. "Hello, there's a small change in plans. I'll be bringing the merchandise. Yeah . . . my partner is indisposed today. Yes . . . I'll be there in a couple of hours. Yes, I know the way. Goodbye."

Smiling, Rosario put his keycard identification in his front shirt pocket . . . and he put J.J.'s keycard identification right behind it in the same pocket. Pulling his carry-on bag behind him, Rosario said goodbye to the ship.

51

The MacAllister family, father and mother and teenage daughter, got into the elevator and rode it to the top deck. But once there the daughter decided the weather was too humid for her hair and convinced her mother and father to go back down to one of the inside restaurants for breakfast.

The family returned to the elevator and pushed the button for the lower deck. As they traveled down through the ship, the daughter sniffed. Something smelled funny she told her parents. Leaning back against the elevator wall she suddenly gave a little shriek and jumped away from the wall.

"It's wet," she said.

Her father looked at the red liquid running down the wall from the top of the elevator. He leaned in closer and, as the elevator stopped and the doors opened, he proclaimed, "That's blood."

His daughter shrieked louder this time. His wife joined in with a full-throated scream. A ship employee was summoned. He in turn summoned a ship's officer, who called for Maintenance. Maintenance brought a ladder and climbed up through a trapdoor in the roof of the elevator . . . and promptly brought up his breakfast at the sight that greeted his eyes on the top of the elevator.

Not only was J.J. dead; he was quite crushed from being caught between the top of the elevator and the top of the elevator shaft.

An inspection of the body left everyone puzzled, since the man had no identification on him. An accounting of everyone on the ship, passengers and crew, was begun immediately.

52

A housekeeping maid pushing her cart filled with dirty laundry down the corridor on an upper deck noticed a door card lying on the floor outside a suite. She saw that the side of the card that was facing up read "Service Required". Not quite sure what to do, she took out her master keycard and opened the door.

"Housekeeping," she called as she stepped in, while at the same time knocking lightly on the door. "Do you need something?"

Then she screamed. And then she almost fainted, but she managed to get back out into the corridor where she used her radio to call her supervisor to report that she had just found a dead body in one of the suites.

When she told her supervisor the number of the suite, things got quite frantic.

சு கல

When the second death was reported to Captain Rivera, he went back to his office and made a direct call to the Chairman of the Board of the cruise line. He was on the phone for several minutes and when he had hung up he sagged back in his chair.

The Captain sat and thought for a minute before pulling himself upright. He picked up his phone again and dialed Information. He then dialed the number he had received from Information and waited for his call to be answered.

"Hello? Police? Yes, this is Captain Rivera of *The Queen of the Islands*. We're docked at the wharf here in Hilo. I need to report a murder . . . maybe two murders. Yes. Yes. All right, please ask your men not to come with red lights flashing and sirens wailing. I want to keep as much of this from our passengers as possible. Yes, I'll meet your men as soon as they get here."

Captain Rivera hung up his desk phone. He reviewed once more just how long he had to continue to work before he could retire.

53

Lori closed her cellphone and turned back to her sisters and Koakane.

"Okay, I got us a van. That should hold all of our luggage."

"Jus' barely, I bet," muttered Koakane from where he sat on the couch, his arm around Teri's shoulder. She elbowed him lightly.

"Well," said Haunani, "we might as well go get some breakfast. It's paid for."

The Pono women, and Koakane, trooped out of Haunani's suite and made their way to the restaurant. On their way they passed a crowd of curious people hanging around the elevators.

Their group was quickly seated in the restaurant, placed their orders and settled in to enjoy their last meal on the ship.

Koakane noticed a great deal of whispering going on among the crew, but decided to ignore it since he and the women were leaving soon. Nothing to do with them, anyway, he thought.

54

Rosario caught a glimpse of the Pono family group as they headed into the restaurant for breakfast. He nodded to himself. Let them take their time, he could wait.

Using one of the forward elevators, Rosario dropped down to the deck where the gangplank was already set up.

"Hey, man, how come you get to go ashore?" one of the men working the gangplank asked. He held a barcode scanner in one hand and a clipboard in the other.

With an engaging smile Rosario said, "I built up my shore leave an' now I gonna use some of it. Look out all you hula maidens."

The other man laughed and extended the barcode scanner.

Rosario slid J.J.'s keycard out of his front shirt pocket and held it out for the gangplank worker to read with the scanner in his hand. Rosario kept most of the card covered with his thumb but left the barcode visible. The scanner read the barcode and duly noted that passenger Ted Brinder had exited the ship.

Rosario walked down the gangplank and out onto the wharf. As he passed trash can he flicked Ted Brinder's keycard into it, after first wiping it clean of prints.

It was truly a beautiful day in Hilo . . . and would only get better.

80CR

As Rosario stepped off the gangplank and onto the wharf, two police officers stepped up to the men overseeing the gangplank.

"We'll take over now," one of the officers said. "Just show us how to use that thing," he indicated the barcode scanner in the one man's hand, "but hang around a bit in case we need to ask you any questions."

⁎⁏

"Here you go, sir. Just sign here."

Rosario signed and pocketed the rental car keys.

"Thank you," he said lifting his bag off the floor.

"Do you need a map?" the rental car agency man asked.

"No, thank you," Rosario answered, "I know just where I'm going.

"Well, have a good day."

"I will," said Rosario, "I certainly will."

Rosario opened the door of the small trailer that sat on the end of the dock. The unimaginative sign on it read *Hilo Rental Cars*. He walked down the steps and over to the rental car that matched the keys he'd been given. A blue Nissan Versa. Small, but all he needed for today. There were only eight cars left, the rest having been snatched up quickly by ship's passengers eager to get out and about on the Big Island. Along with the eight remaining cars, there was one van. A white Nissan Quest.

Rosario guessed that if the Pono family was going to rent car, that would be the one they picked.

Actually it didn't matter to Rosario. He got into his Versa, pulled out and made his way down the wharf to a spot where he could park, legally, and watch the people coming off the ship. He opened the car windows, adjusted the rear view and side view mirrors so that he could see even when slumped back in his seat. Rosario settled down to wait.

55

Captain Rivera welcomed the police sergeant and two other officers to the office section of his cabin.

"Sorry we have to meet like this, I'm Sergeant Akamai and these are Officers Lum and Fertado."

Captain Rivera gestured the three police officers to seats and took his own seat behind his desk.

"This is very troubling, Sergeant. We have had deaths before on our ship, but never a murder . . . certainly not two. I hope you and your men can treat this matter discreetly."

"We'll do what we can to avoid upsetting your passengers . . . but we are looking for a murderer. And he's on this ship."

But he wasn't.

56

The women of the Pono family, accompanied by Koakane, got off the elevator and headed for the gangplank. They had managed to gather all their suitcases and bags and were carrying them with them. Koakane had his airline carry-on bag in one hand and Teri's in the other. Teri had insisted that she and she alone would carry the two shopping bags filled with beef jerky from Las Vegas. For some reason they felt heavier than the last time she had lifted them.

At the gangplank two uniformed police officers waited, along with two members of the ship's crew.

The women all produced their keycards which were scanned and then returned to them.

"We really don't need these anymore," said Shari, we're home.

"Oh, keep it, makes a nice souvenir," Lori said.

The women started to make their way down the gangplank. Koakane had to put down his two bags in order to retrieve his keycard from his pocket.

One of the police officers scanned it with the barcode scanner. He stared at the result, and then took a folded piece of paper out of his pocket, unfolded it and read it carefully.

"Koakane Kealoha?"

"Yes, that's me."

"I'm sorry, you need to come with us," the first officer said as the other moved in behind Koakane.

"Bring your bags with you," the officer behind Koakane said.

"Okay, but can you tell me why?"

The women had stopped on the gangplank and were looking back at Koakane with the two policemen.

"Our sergeant would like to talk with you," the first officer said. "Just some routine questions."

Koakane looked down at the women on the gangplank.

Teri started to walk back up.

Koakane waved at her.

"No, you go on. I'll join up with you after I get this straightened out. Go on."

Haunani touched Teri's shoulder and gently pulled her down the gangplank.

Teri kept looking back at the ship as she and her sisters and mother walked down the dock toward the rental car trailer.

ↄↃ

From his seat in his rental car, Rosario saw the women walking along the dock. He watched them go into the rental car trailer, and, then, a few minutes later he saw them come out, walk over to a Nissan van and load their luggage into the back. But he carefully noted that Teri got into the front passenger seat. And that she kept the two shopping bags with her.

As the women drove off they missed seeing the small blue Nissan Versa that pulled out after them and followed them out onto Highway 11, the Hawaii Belt Road.

₧₨

With Shari driving Teri was forced to stay alert. Her sister was a little unpredictable in many ways, and her driving habits were one of those ways.

Lori and Haunani sat in the middle section seats, holding firmly onto each other's hand and muttering silent advice to Shari. *Slow down. Get off the shoulder. Watch the cars coming toward us.*

Shari however was blissfully unaware of her family's concerns and kept up a steady stream of one-sided talk.

"Well, that was some trip. I could do it again. I would have liked to have more time to talk with some of the younger men on the ship. Did you see how many old people there were? Then again, an older man with a lot of money might not make such a bad date," turning around to look in the back seat, Shari added, "Are you okay back there, Mom? If you wanted I could pull over and you could change places with Teri."

Haunani shook her head no and only replied, "Is okay, I'm fine. Just keep your eyes on the road. Please, just watch the road. Dangerous this belt road at times."

Shari huffed and turned back toward the front.

"Don't worry, I can drive this road with my eyes closed."

"But let's not try it today," Lori said.

57

With one officer in front and one behind, Koakane entered the Ship Captain's office and stopped immediately when he saw who else was in the office.

"Hey, Sergeant Akamai, howzit?"

The sergeant stepped over and shook Koakane's hand.

"How you doing, Koakane?"

"Just fine, until your boys wouldn't let me get off the ship."

Sergeant Akamai gestured to a chair and, once Koakane was seated, the sergeant pulled a chair close to Koakane's and sat down himself.

"So . . . why am I here?" Koakane asked.

"I need to find out what you know about the two murders."

"Murders? What murders?"

"Two people were killed onboard just recently," Sergeant Akamai said as he leaned back in his chair, "and you had an encounter with one of them."

When Koakane looked puzzled, the sergeant continued, "A lot of people saw you get really angry with Marilyn Hardin. You even threatened her. Now she's dead. Any connection there?"

"She's dead? How?"

When the sergeant didn't say anything further, Koakane said, "And because I yelled at her, you think I killed her? Listen, I won't shed any tears over that woman's grave . . . but I did not kill her."

"Where did you go after your show was over?"

"I, and Haunani and her daughters, went to dinner. Then we went back to our cabins."

"Can anyone verify that?"

Koakane didn't answer.

"You need some proof of your whereabouts, otherwise I might need to hold you over at the station."

After an internal struggle, Koakane finally said, "Yes, I've got someone who can verify where I was all last night."

"Who?"

"Teri. Teri Pono."

58

While Rosario was concentrating on following the women of the Pono family down by Hilo, Greyson tiptoed out of Tommy's apartment in Kona. He didn't bother looking at Tommy, sprawled on his bed, a smile on his face reflecting the pleasant dreams he was having.

Greyson went into the small apartment kitchen, drank half of a large bottle of orange juice, replaced the bottle and grabbed two water bottles from the refrigerator. The bottles went into his carry-on bag, along with the lei niho. Hoisting the bag onto his shoulder Greyson picked Tommy's car keys out of the Koa wood bowl on a small table by the front door. He didn't figure that Tommy might miss his car, and Greyson promised himself that he'd fill the tank with gas when he got done later today.

Two minutes later he was pulling out of the apartment complex parking lot and heading for the road that led up to Mauna Loa. He'd been on the mountain many times, hiking and exploring it. He knew just where some hidden caves were, if no one else had found them.

ഔൽ

In order to borrow his sister's car, Vincent had to drive her to her job and agree to pick her up when she was finished for the day.

"An' you gonna buy dinner too," she told him through the window when he let her off.

"Okay, okay . . . no bus' my chops. That's why I don't come over her more often."

"Sure, an' when you do come over you only want something. So, don' forget, buy dinner . . . and for your nephew too."

"Yeah, yeah," Vincent called out as he drove away, and added in a whisper, "Zippy's plenty good enough."

A few minutes later he was heading up to the Nu'uanu Valley.

Lots of caves up there, he thought to himself.

🙰

Over on Maui, Palani assured his auntie that he'd be leaving later that day. No, he wasn't staying. Yes, he'd be careful with her car. Yes, he'd put gas in it. No, he wasn't in any trouble.

He almost started to tell her that he was helping the islands, restoring the aina. Then he remembered Vincent telling them how important it was to keep all their activities secret. So he just took the keys from his auntie's outstretched hand, kissed her on the cheek and went to warm up the car in the carport outside.

Leaving Kahului behind, Palani headed for the Iao Valley. He hoped he would get there before the tourist buses started their daily circuit of the island. He knew a cave up the valley. He hoped that it was still there and hadn't either fallen in or been found by others.

59

"Okay, Koakane, I don't think we have any more to talk about with you," said Sergeant Akamai.

"I'm free to go?"

"Yep."

"One problem, Sergeant. Haunani and her daughters will have picked up their rental car by now and will be headed home. I got no wheels. Do you suppose one of your men could give me a ride at least into Kona? Maybe drop me off at my house so I can pick up my truck?"

Sergeant Akamai's forehead wrinkled as he thought.

"Okay," he said with a nod of his head, "I need to go to Kona myself. The techs and detectives can keep on working while I'm gone, so, yes, I'll give you a lift over to Kona."

"Mahalo," Koakane said, "who knows, maybe we can even catch up with the women and then I can ride with them."

80Q8

His carry-on bag in one hand and Teri's in the other, Koakane followed Sergeant Akamai down the gangplank. They walked the length of the dock to where the sergeant had parked his unmarked Ford Crown Victoria. Climbing in, Big Ed opened the windows and turned on the air conditioning to blow out the hot air that had accumulated since he had parked it earlier.

Koakane put his two bags in the back seat and got into the front passenger seat. Sitting there he felt something press against the back of his calves. Looking down he saw the twelve-gauge pump shotgun in a rack. He glanced at Big Ed and saw a grin on his face.

"Always gotta have an advantage," Big Ed said as he slipped the car into gear and pulled out.

Big Ed drove quickly and efficiently through traffic, heading for the Hawaii Belt Road. He passed car after car. But nowhere did he see the blue van with the women of the Pono family.

60

Rosario saw the blue van ahead of him on the Belt Road. He quickly caught up to it and soon was just a car length behind them. He checked his rearview mirror, nothing behind him for a long way. The shoulder along this stretch of the road was good. Solid and dry right now. Pushing down on the gas pedal, Rosario swung out to pass, pleased to see no cars in the oncoming lane.

"Bakatare," Shari said as she swerved to the right.

The little blue Nissan Versa pulled around their van, and pulled in front of them. And promptly tapped its brakes.

Shari had no choice; she either had to slow down or rear end the little car.

The little car stayed in front of the van and braked some more. Then it dropped back to the left and braked even more.

The only way to avoid it was for Shari to pull over to the shoulder and stop. The little blue car pulled in right in front of the van and its driver's side door opened.

Rosario leapt out and, leaving his car running, raced back to the front passenger side door of the van. He yanked it open.

His knife in his hand Rosario confronted Teri.

"Give me those bags," he demanded. And to reinforce his demand Rosario put the point of his knife up to Teri's breast.

"What? Rosario? What are you doing?"

"Give me the bags," Rosario again demanded, pushing the knife point forward and pricking Teri's breast.

"Here, take them," Teri said reaching down and pulling the bags off the floor.

Rosario grabbed the two bags with one hand. He dropped them onto the shoulder of the highway and turned his attention to Shari.

"Keys," he said, "give me the keys."

Shari quickly removed the keys from the ignition and passed them to Rosario's outstretched hand.

Backing away from the van, Rosario tossed the keys back into the tall grass alongside the shoulder. Waving his knife for emphasis, he picked up the two shopping bags and ran back to his car. He threw the bags in through the driver side door, and jumped into the seat.

The women watched as Rosario's blue car spun its wheels and threw gravel over their van. Then it pulled out onto the highway and sped away.

"Did anyone get his license number?" Lori asked from the middle seat section.

"No," Teri said rubbing her breast, "but I got a good look at his knife."

Shari heaved a sigh, looked back in the sideview mirror and got out of the van.

"Where are you going?" asked Teri.

"To get the keys, I saw where he threw them," said Shari.

Haunani finally spoke up, "That little buggah must really like beef jerky."

With the tension broken the women all laughed for the next two minutes.

$$\mathcal{SO}\mathcal{CR}$$

They stopped laughing when the unmarked police car pulled up behind them and Koakane and Sergeant Akamai got out.

61

Sergeant Akamai and Koakane walked quickly up to the women's van.

Koakane and Teri hugged while Sergeant Akamai assessed the scene and turned to Haunani.

"Haunani."

"Big Ed."

"So, what happened here?"

Haunani, joined by her daughters, related the events of just a short while ago. They also told him about the rest of their trip and Haunani mentioned the theft of her good luck plastic frog while they were in Las Vegas.

"But what we can't figure out is why that buggah wanted to steal Teri's beef jerky," Haunani concluded.

The reason became clear to Sergeant Akamai at that instant.

"The jewels."

"What jewels," Haunani, Shari, Lori and Teri all chorused.

So Sergeant Akamai told them about the murder of Marilyn Hardin ("Oh, da poor lady") and about the theft of her jewels ("They're worth *how* much?").

"Sorry," Sergeant Akamai said, "I have to catch up with that man. He's probably heading for the Kona airport." And with that Sergeant Akamai turned and jogged back to his car, pulled the bags Koakane had been carrying out of the car and dumped them on the highway, got behind the wheel, turned on his lights and siren, and pulled out onto the highway heading toward Kona.

Koakane, Teri, Haunani and Lori watched him pull away and within seconds disappear from view up the Belt Road.

"Found 'em," Shari called.

The rest of the family turned to see her standing amongst the roadside weeds, holding the van's keys up in the air triumphantly.

"Told you I saw where that jerk threw 'em. Let's get going."

After loading the last luggage in the back, the group repositioned itself in the van. Shari driving; Haunani in the front passenger seat; Teri, Koakane and Lori in the back; Teri in the middle with Koakane next to her with his arm draped over her shoulders.

"Slow down," Haunani instructed Shari. "Big Ed's driving the police car, not you."

62

Sergeant Akamai flew along the Belt Road, zipping past all the little towns and subdivisions along the way. He radioed in that he was heading for the Kona International Airport and that he was in pursuit of a suspected thief and murderer. The Belt Road became the Mamalahoa Highway, which in turn became the Kuakini Highway and finally, as he passed Kailua Kona, turned into the Queen Ka'ahumanu Highway.

The sergeant felt himself closing in on Rosario. With the airport exit only a short distance ahead the adrenalin began to build up in his body.

63

Two minutes before Sergeant Akamai passed Kailua Kona, Rosario turned off the highway, slowed down and headed toward Ali'i Drive. Driving slowly, he found the address he was looking for and, without too much trouble, a parking space around the corner from a shop with a sign on the door reading:

ANTIQUES AND COLLECTIBLES
Specializing in Hawai`iana
Sherman Richards, Proprietor

After parking and locking his car, Rosario made his way around the corner while carrying the two shopping bags filled with packages of beef jerky. He set one bag down while he opened the door, picked it back up and entered the shop. Rosario kicked the door shut behind him. He stood for a moment in the shop entrance, allowing his eyes to adjust to the dim light inside.

"Hey," he called, "anybody here?"

A man of medium height, haole, slightly overweight, hair slicked back and greasy-looking, appeared out of the shadows.

"Can I help you?"

"You Richards?"

"Yes, I'm Sherman Richards, proprietor. And you are?"

"I'm from the ship . . . with the goods," Rosario said as he hoisted the two shopping bags up for Sherman Richards to observe.

"Ahhh," said Richards, "Perhaps we should move away from the front of the shop," and he stepped to one side as he indicated that Rosario should go past him. As Rosario moved along the path Richards had indicated, Richards moved to the front door of the shop, locked it and turned the sign over from 'Open' to 'Closed'. He then followed Rosario.

Just a little way in there was an empty table. Rosario placed the two shopping bags on it and turned back to Richards.

"Please show me the merchandise," said Richards.

Rosario stared at Richards for a moment, nodded and began pulling the packages of beef jerky from the two bags. Richards waited patiently. Rosario shoved all the beef jerky packages to one end of the table and finally brought out the velvet bags containing Marilyn Hardin's jewelry.

Richards stepped forward, took hold of one of the jewelry bags and dumped the contents out onto the table. He sucked in his breath slightly as the diamonds sparkled in a stray beam of light.

"Very nice," Richards said.

"Now let's see my money," said Rosario.

Richards nodded and walked back to a small glassed-in office at the side of the store. He went inside, picked up a large manila envelope and came back out.

Walking over to where Rosario stood, Richards plunked the envelope down on the table. At that point another man emerged from the shadows. A hulking figure, large and muscular. His skin color and facial features identified him as a local.

Rosario's forehead wrinkled at the appearance of this man. He looked back and forth from Richards to the other man.

"Well?" Richards said, "there's your money."

Continually turning his head to keep track of the two men, Rosario picked up the manila envelope and looked inside. He dumped the contents onto the table.

"Don't look like two hundred thousand to me," he said.

"It's not. It's fifty thousand," said Richards.

"Our deal was for two hundred, not fifty."

"Our deal didn't include murder," said Richards. "It's on the morning news already. The lady was killed on the ship. Theft is one thing, murder another. This whole thing just got much riskier for me. Fifty thousand is all I'm willing to risk."

Rosario realized that he didn't know another fence to handle the jewels and pay him the money he wanted. J.J. did, but he was dead.

Rosario backed up so that he could watch both men at the same time easier. He slipped his right hand into his pants pocket.

"Our deal is for two hundred, not fifty. You need to come up with the rest of it right now."

Sherman Richards exhaled with frustration.

"I don't have that much money here right now. I had to work to get together the fifty thousand. You take that fifty. Let me know when you find someplace to lie low and I'll send you another fifty after I get rid of the merchandise."

Rosario considered the offer. Half what they'd initially agreed upon, but no need to split it with J.J. But this guy was right, it was riskier now . . . and he, Rosario, was the one risking it all.

"No, I'll tell you what I'll do. I'll take the fifty now, and when you pull together another fifty I'll get the jewels back to you."

Richards sighed.

"No, that's not the way it's going to happen," Richards said and took a step toward Rosario.

Rosario pulled his knife from his pocket, snapped it open and waved it between Richards and the other man.

"Yes, I think that's just the way it is going to happen," said Rosario.

Richards' eyes flicked toward his assistant. Rosario's eyes followed Richards' and thus he didn't see the gun that Richards pulled from his back pocket. Richards took a step closer to Rosario, raised the gun and, as Rosario turned back toward Richards, Richards fired one shot into Rosario's forehead. Rosario collapsed like a puppet whose strings had been cut. His knife fell from his hand and clattered on the floor.

Richards put his gun down on the table. He looked through all the velvet jewelry bags, selected two and headed for the back storeroom where he had a secret closet. Pausing, he turned back to his assistant.

"Geoffrey, leave everything there alone. Go unlock the front door and then call the police. Tell them there's been a shooting and they should get here quick. Then hang up. Got that?"

"Sure, no problem," looking down at the blood still leaking out onto the floor from the wound in Rosario's head, Geoffrey said, "I get da mop an' da bucket?"

"No, not until after the police leave. Now get busy with the things I told you to do. And remember, all you saw was this turd waving a knife around and threatening both you and me with it. You don't know why he came here or what he wanted."

Geoffrey went toward the front door. Richards went into the back storeroom, and closed the door behind him. It would have upset him to find out that Geoffrey already knew about his boss's secret closet. But Geoffrey wasn't about to let that secret out.

64

Spread out across the islands, the three members of the Hawaiian Sovereignty splinter group, Greyson, Vincent and Palani, set off on their separate missions.

Vincent borrowed his sister's car again, and left a note telling her this. He drove up Highway 61 toward the Pali. Turning off the highway at one point, he paralleled it on side streets gradually drawing away from the highway and into the mountains. The streets grew narrower, the houses smaller and farther apart. He went from paved to unpaved. No more houses. Vincent recognized the signs of pakalolo cultivation and made sure to keep on moving along the dirt road. Soon it was just two ruts leading further up into the mountains. When even the ruts ran out he drove on another hundred yards and parked the car in the midst of tall grass and old trees. He knew that if she were here, Beatrice would really be pissed.

So, I piss her off before, and gonna piss her off again, probably.

It was many years since Vincent had been here but his feet seemed to remember the way. He put his bag with the lei niho down, took out a water bottle and drank. Looking up at the cliffs ahead of him he shook his head, sighed, drank once more and replaced the bottle. Two more in the bag. *Gonna need those,* he thought. He began walking.

☙❧

Greyson figured he had the easiest mission as he drove his car up to the north end of the island. His destination was an old and burned out part of the volcano, Pu'u Mamo, near to Hawi. He was driving along Highway 270, the Queen Ka'ahumanu Highway and was enjoying himself. This was almost like a vacation. Greyson looked out to sea, smiling at the sight of the bright blue water and the many whitecaps. As he passed the Kapaa Beach Park Road he saw a tourist sign on his right, noting that the birthplace of King Kamehameha lay ahead.

A chill ran down his spine and made his whole body shake. For a moment he worried that he might lose control of his car. The moment passed. Greyson took a deep breath and realized that this was not a vacation day.

℘℧

Palani promised once more to put gas in his auntie's car. Then he headed out for Iao Valley. He arrived before the first tourist bus of the day pulled up. Grabbing his carry-on bag with the lei niho, three water bottles and a flashlight inside, he began hiking up the path that ran beside the Iao Stream. It was a bubbling cheerful stream that flowed down from the Iao Needle far above, running over the rocks and sparkling in the sunlight. But Palani knew that at one time, years ago, the water had run red with the blood of the warriors killed in a battle here. And some parts of the stream had been blocked with the bodies of those same warriors. It had been a fierce battle, a battle for the island of Maui and Kamehameha had won that battle.

It was a beautiful place, and Palani also knew that many royal persons, many Ali'i were buried in the valley, hidden away in caves.

He was panting now, his breathing rough from the exertion of climbing toward the Iao Needle. He could see the Needle far above him. Someone had once told him that the Iao Needle was taller than the Eiffel Tower. He'd never been to France, but he could certainly see that the Needle was tremendously high.

Palani reached a familiar spot on the trail, a spot he had found years ago when hiking up the valley with his uncle, the uncle who had died and left his wife alone on Maui. Looking back down the trail he saw no one following him. Looking ahead he saw no early hikers on their way back down. He listened, intently and heard only the sound of the stream on its way down to the valley below.

Stepping off the trail he pushed gently through the vegetation that flanked the trail. He made it a point to replace the vines and leaves and branches so as not to let anyone know that he had entered here. Moving forward stealthily he found his way to where the ground rose up slightly. Palani stopped and listened and looked around again. Then, stepping forward, he gently pulled apart the vegetation just enough to reveal the small opening of a cave. Getting down on his hands and knees, he took the flashlight from his bag and wriggled in through the cave mouth.

65

Across the water and over at the Kona International Airport, Sergeant Akamai pulled up to the red curb and parked behind a marked police car. Standing on the sidewalk beside it was a young policeman.

"Hey, Lawrence, where is he?"

"Hey, Sarge. No see 'um. No little blue car with jus' a driver pull in here. All the rental agencies been notified."

"Shoot," said Sergeant Akamai. "He wasn't that far ahead of me. He should be here."

Just then the radio in the marked car crackled with the information that there had been a shooting in Kona, at an antiques store. The hair on the back of Sergeant Akamai's neck stood up.

"Lawrence, you stay here . . . just in case he still shows up."

"Where you going, Sarge?"

"I know that store and I know the owner. I think maybe our man had a different destination."

Sergeant Akamai stepped back around to the driver's side door of his car.

"Look, Lawrence, give the TSA guys all the info we have. If this guy doesn't turn up in an hour, call in and ask Dispatch where you should go."

And with that Sergeant Akamai hopped back into his car, pulled smoothly away from the curb and accelerated along the airport road and back up to the highway. He turned right, put on his flashers and raced toward Kona, swearing creatively the whole way.

66

Sergeant Akamai pulled up next to a fire hydrant across the street from the antique store. He got out of his car, locking the door behind him. He crossed the street without benefit of crosswalk. No one was inclined to debate the right of a man wearing a badge, and a gun, to cross the street anywhere he pleased.

The sergeant said hello to a patrolman stationed at the front door of the shop.

"Crime scene guys inside?"

"Yeah, been here about twenty minutes so far."

Big Ed grunted, pulled the door open and went inside. He paused to allow his eyes to adjust to the gloom of the store. There were lights on, but they failed to push back the darkness. Big Ed guessed that the low light made it hard for buyers to see any flaws in the merchandise.

Once his eyes had adjusted he made his way toward the center of the store. He stopped and took in the sight of the body on the floor, blood spread out around the head like a halo. One detective was standing off to the side talking with Sherman Richards and taking notes. A bulky local man stood behind Richards' right shoulder, his mouth clamped tightly shut. A second detective crouched beside the body poking at the dead man's pockets.

"Jerry," Sergeant Akamai said.

"Big Ed," the second detective replied without turning around.

"What's it look like?"

"Fairly straightforward. Guy tries to sell some jewelry to the store owner. They argue. Guy pulls a knife. Store owner pulls a gun and shoots the guy when he lunges with the knife."

"Guess the guy never heard the old saying, 'Never bring a knife to a gunfight'."

"Guess not," Jerry said standing up and stretching his back. "There's the stuff he brought," and he indicated items on a glass-topped display case behind the body.

Sergeant Akamai stepped around the body and over to the display case. Arranged along the glass top were two empty shopping bags bearing the logo of a shop in Las Vegas. With them was a stack of beef jerky bags, all varieties. Then he saw the velvet bags, opened and with the jewelry that they had held piled on top of each bag. Stepping closer Big Ed pulled out his phone, tapped on it a bit and then looked at the list he had brought up. His hunch had been right, there were at least two bags of jewelry missing.

Just then Big Ed's eye was caught by a small green object next to the jewelry. A small green plastic frog.

"Jerry, where you find this frog?"

Jerry squinted as he leaned forward over the body to see what Big Ed was talking about.

"Oh, that? It was in one of the jewelry bags. Thought it was alive at first . . . made me jump."

Sergeant Akamai picked up the frog, inspected it and then dialed a number from his phone's directory.

"Teri? Think I found something of yours. Where are you people? Uh-huh. Okay. Well, turn around and head back to Kona. Sherman Richards' antique store. Okay. See you."

Sergeant Akamai hung up his phone and stood for a minute in thought. *How did that plastic frog wind up in one of those jewelry bags? Didn't Haunani mention that it had been stolen from her in Las Vegas?*

67

The three men of the Hawaiian Sovereignty splinter group each struggled to complete their task of returning the mana to the islands.

Greyson had parked his car off the road and hiked in to the old volcano. It wasn't readily apparent that this large earth mound had once been a volcano since it had collapsed in on itself and did not have a caldera. But it had once been an offshoot of the larger volcanos on the island.

Greyson walked around the base until he found what he was looking for. A small gouge in the side of the mound, not really a valley, ran partway up one side. Because it seemed to go nowhere, and because it became quite steep as it got higher, few people explored it. But Greyson had been here before.

He climbed the side of the volcano making his way up the small valley. As he got near the top he had to pull himself along on his hands and knees. Finally, he reached a flat spot, just large enough for him to sit down, next to a crack in the side of the volcano. The crack was about three feet high and just under two feet wide. Inside was darkness.

Greyson had been inside this crack once before, and the memories made him shiver again. He thought about going in and leaving the lei mano inside the volcano. He turned, got up on his knees and leaned into the crack. A cold draught of air met him head-on. Greyson pulled back. He set his bag down in front of him and thought.

Greyson tried once more to lean into the crack, to peer into the heart of the ancient volcano. Once more a cold draught of air seemed to blow him back.

Opening his bag, Greyson reached in and pulled out the lei mano he had carried all this way. He held them in his hand while he contemplated his next actions.

"Okay," Greyson called into the dark crack, "you don't want me coming in. Fine. Here, take these back and guard them."

And with that Greyson threw the lei mano as far into the darkness as he was able. The lei mano made no sound as they vanished from sight.

Scrambling backwards, Greyson retreated hastily down the side of the ancient volcano, moved quickly to where he had left his car parked, got in and drove away.

Back up at the crack in the ancient volcano, a warm breeze sighed softly from out of the darkness.

He was several miles away before Greyson began to breathe normally once again.

ഇരു

Vincent had sweat through his shirt but kept it on as protection from the fierce sun above. When he reached the base of the cliffs he stopped, drank half of one water bottle, replaced it in his bag and craned his neck to look above him.

Perfectly hidden, he thought.

Far above him the jagged cliff seemed unbroken. But Vincent, having been here before, knew that the cliff was undercut and that a ledge lay hidden up there. Invisible from both above and below, the only way to see it was to climb up to it.

So he did.

It was a tricky climb and twice his heart stopped when rock gave way beneath his foot and he was forced to claw for a handhold.

But he reached the ledge. The cliff came down over the ledge like a curtain and left only two feet or so of opening. Vincent rolled through the opening and wound up with his face inches from a grinning skull. Scattered around on the ledge, either by the forces of nature or scavengers, were a number of skulls, long bones of leg and arm and the fragments of lauhala baskets. The ledge continued on into the mountain becoming a low cave, one that Vincent could enter only on his belly. As his eyes adjusted to the darkness of this cave Vincent saw more white bones and skulls.

Vincent took a deep breath and crawled forward, dragging his bag behind him. When he could force himself to go no further forward he pulled his bag up with him, unzipped it and took out the lei niho inside. Carefully he placed the lei niho around on the floor of the cave. Unable to turn around he crawled backwards pulling his bag after him.

Vincent crawled out of the cave and back onto the ledge. He sat on the ledge, his head bent while still touching the roof of the ledge. Vincent pulled the half-empty water bottle from his bag, drank the rest of it and replaced the empty bottle in the bag.

After breathing deeply for a few minutes Vincent began to make his way back down to the valley below. He felt light and wanted to sing, but was afraid of calling attention to himself while he was still climbing down.

Once he reached the foot of the cliff though, he broke into song. And he sang, old songs, new songs, songs he made up as he walked back to where he had left his sister's car.

And he cursed when he saw her car . . . the windshield plastered with mud. And written in mud on the other windows,

No Come HERE.

The pakalolo growers had spoken.

It took him all the rest of his water to clean the windows, and when he drove away he was exceedingly thirsty. But content.

❧ ❧

Palani had only moved a little way into the cave before he was forced to turn on the flashlight he'd brought with him in his carry-on bag. Now he shone it around the inside of the cave and was immediately sorry that he had done so.

The flashlight's beam only served to show him how small the cave, really just a hole in the ground, was. It was formed of lava rock but the floor was mostly dirt. Centuries old dirt. His flashlight's beam couldn't penetrate to the end of the cave, if there was an end. This was about as far as he had ever gone into the cave, but now he felt the need to go farther.

As he progressed the weight of the mountain above him seemed to press down on him. The tunnel got narrower and narrower.

Just as Palani thought that this was as far as he should go, his left shoulder brushed the wall and caused a very small avalanche of rocks. His heart stopped as he thought he was about to be buried alive in this cave.

The rocks stopped moving and silence came again.

Palani trained his flashlight on the side wall and recognized that the rocks were placed there purposefully. They walled up a hole in the side of the cave. Palani scrambled backwards a little and began carefully pulling the rocks out of the hole. He enlarged the opening until it was wide enough for him to see in.

Shining his flashlight through the opening, Palani saw another cave. Taller than the one he was in, it formed a bubble. Inside this cave he saw objects, man-made ones.

By twisting and turning Palani was able to crawl into this bubble cave. Once inside he was able to sit up, his head just grazing the ceiling. The first object he saw in the light from his flashlight made his heart stop again.

It was about a foot high, covered in feathers, with two eyes made of seashell and a mouth lined with dog's teeth. It looked as if it might bite him.

Looking around slowly Palani saw dried lauhala wrapped around things . . . things that he knew to be bones and skulls of olden days Ali'i. He saw a canoe paddle, broken in half so that whoever brought it in was able to get it through the opening and into this chamber. He saw weapons, formed from koa wood and studded with shark teeth. And he saw gourds and bowls, finely formed.

Turning his head further to the side, Palani fell backwards away from a row of grinning skulls on a shelf carved into the lava rock.

Suddenly he wanted to get away.

But first he had his mission to complete.

Reaching back out through the opening in the rock wall, Palani pulled his carry-on into the bubble with him. Swiftly he removed the lei niho from his bag and spread them out in the bubble cave. When he had placed them all carefully, he backed out of the bubble cave and back into the tunnel.

Palani piled the rocks back up in the opening until it was completely walled off. Then, taking a bottle of water from his carry-on, he mixed the water with the dirt of the cave floor and used the resulting mud to fill in the gaps of the rocks. He smoothed everything out until he was satisfied that once dry the opening to the bubble cave would be hidden once more.

It seemed to take forever for him to crawl backwards out of the tunnel. And once outside he gathered more rocks and brush to hide the cave entrance.

Drinking the last of his water, Palani looked about carefully and, seeing no one either coming up or down the path, he moved quickly to return to his Auntie's car.

Once down at the car he looked back up the valley and was pleased to see the top of the Iao Valley Needle shining in the sunlight.

68

Teri's phone rang just as their car was passing the West Hawaii Veteran's Cemetery.

"Hello? Oh, hi Sergeant Akamai. What? That too? Where did you find them? Uh-huh. Yes. Yes. We're on our way."

Clicking off her phone Teri leaned forward and spoke to Shari.

"Turn around. We have to go back to Kona."

"Why?"

Everyone in the car was focused on Teri now.

"That was Sergeant Akamai."

"Yeah, we know, we heard."

"That guy from the ship, the Cabin Steward, he's dead. Shot in the antique store in Kona. You know the one. Sherman Richards' store. And they found my bags of beef jerky there."

Teri turned to Haunani.

"Mom, they found your lucky frog with the beef jerky."

"All right," Haunani said, "now my luck's gonna come back."

Teri turned back to Shari.

"Turn around, we have to go get our stuff back."

Shari skidded to a stop along the side of the highway. She pulled U-turn back toward Kona, coming entirely too close to the oncoming traffic as far as everyone in the van was concerned.

The group raced toward Kona eyes shut and holding on for dear life.

ॐ

Since Shari had always had more luck than common sense, she found a parking spot just around the corner from Sherman Richards' antique store.

The little group piled out of the van, walked quickly around the corner, convinced the police officer in front of the store that they had urgent business inside and squeezed through the front door.

"Aloha, Sergeant Akamai," Teri called.

"Hey, Big Ed, where's my frog?" Haunani asked.

They halted at the chalked outline of a body on the floor, blood still caked around it.

"Rosario?" said Teri.

Big Ed pushed off from the glass display case he had been leaning against. Sherman Richards, standing a little off to the side, winced as the case protested at the shift in weight.

"Yep. Had Ms. Hardin's jewels, most of them anyway, with him. Richards says he tried to sell them to him. Pulled a knife when he couldn't make a deal and got himself shot. At least," Big Ed looked over at Richards, "that's the story we have . . . so far."

Richards pulled a face, but declined to comment.

"Oh," said Teri, "there's my jerky," and she walked around the chalk outline and over to where her shopping bags sat on the display case.

"And my lucky frog," said Haunani as she followed Teri.

Haunani picked up the little plastic green frog.

"My good luck."

"Not his though," said Big Ed. "We have pictures of your items, you've identified them, so you're free to take them."

Teri picked up her shopping bags and walked back around the outline of Rosario's body.

"Bought yourself a lot of jerky in Vegas?" Big Ed said.

Teri looked Big Ed. Looked at her bags. Grimaced and pulled out two one-pound packages from one of the bags and handed them to Big Ed.

"Oh? For me? Mahalo," said Big Ed.

"Okay? Let's go," Koakane said, "it's been a long day already."

"Time for a . . . *nap*?" said Shari.

As Teri headed for the door she swung a bag full of beef jerky packages into Shari's thigh.

"Oww," Shari protested. "That hurts. I don't think I can drive with that much pain."

"Good," said Koakane as he snatched the car keys from Shari's hand. "Now maybe we'll get home alive."

Koakane held the store's door open as the women exited and headed for the van. As Teri came out he relieved her of her bags and she in turn slipped her arm through his.

Leaning in close she whispered in his ear, "A *nap* sounds awfully good."

69

Back at the Pono Family Hale it no longer looked like an explosion in a department store. Even the suitcases had been returned to storage. Lori had departed for the Queen's Beach Resort Hotel to put in some time going through messages and mail before she had to return to work tomorrow.

Shari was trying on each of the many items of clothing that she had purchased on their trip. Walking by her room earlier Teri had insisted that Shari close her door . . . or at least put on some underwear.

Koakane had departed for his house down in Kona with the promise that he'd be by tomorrow and that he and Teri would celebrate with a nice, quiet dinner down in Kalihiwai.

Haunani had settled down for a nap with her little green frog safely ensconsed on the pillow beside her.

Teri had put all of her things away and should have been heading for a nap in her room. She couldn't figure out why she was still just standing there in the living room, looking around and re-remembering the house she grew up on. So many familiar things placed around this room, this room where so much of the family's lives had unfolded.

Her gaze traveled around the room and finally came to rest upon a painting hanging in the corner. Dark with age and dust, if she hadn't seen it for so many years Teri would not have known what it was. But she had seen it, all her life, and could still recognize the woman in the portrait. Queen Ka'ahumanu.

Teri stepped up to the portrait and brushed at the years of dirt that had accumulated on it. Shaking her head at the little effect her efforts produced, she turned and walked down the hallway to the kitchen, returning a minute later with a kitchen towel with one corner of it dampened. Gently she wiped away some of the grime that covered the queen's face. She was a beautiful woman, but stern. Glancing down at the bottom corner of the portrait, Teri rubbed a little more of the grime away there. A name. She puzzled over it and finally was able to sound it out. Dampier. Dampier? Why did that name have any meaning for her. Who was this artist, and why had this portrait of Queen Ka'ahumanu hung in her family's house all these years.

Teri sighed and decided she'd have to wait until her mother work in order to seek answers to those questions.

70

Francisco pulled his pickup off the highway and onto the shoulder behind Big Ed's Ford Crown Vic. He got out and walked up to the driver side window. Big Ed rolled the window down.

"Evening, Francisco. Ready for your first night?"

"Yep."

"Got your flashlight?"

Francisco held up a black flashlight and clicked it on and off to show that the batteries were working. In his other hand Big Ed noted the large water bottle, condensation on the outside revealing that it had recently come from Francisco's refrigerator.

"Phone?"

Francisco patted a pocket of his pants.

"Okay, let's go," Big Ed said as he got out of his car and locked the doors. Francisco didn't bother locking his truck as there was nothing in it worth stealing. He did flick on the cutoff switch under the dash so that no one could be able to get it started and make off with it.

Together the two men walked about one hundred yards forward. After inspecting the highway in both directions they moved quickly across to the makai side. Once there they pushed through the tall vegetation to find themselves on a well-trodden path leading down to the ocean. They followed the path until they reached a point where all vegetation disappeared and below them was only a narrow strip of sand and then lava rock and tidepools.

Big Ed stopped so suddenly that Francisco nearly ran into him. From the bushes to the side of the path an older Hawaiian man, his skin brown from years of living and working in the sun, stepped out.

"Yeah?" said Big Ed.

"Nothing," said the man. He looked carefully at Francisco, then moved around the two men and set off back up the path and toward the highway.

Big Ed and Francisco stepped off the path and pushed through into the bushes where the older man had come out. They settled down about fifteen feet off the path, in a well-used area that screened them from view while allowing them to look down onto the ocean and the rocks some fifty yards away. Through the bushes they could even see the path they had walked down, but Francisco saw they were well hidden from anyone who might come walking the path. Behind them was a stunted Kiawe tree which helped hide them in its shadow.

The sun dipped and slid beneath the horizon, its rays lighting the clouds for a few more minutes. Soon it was dark.

"Okay," Big Ed whispered as he turned toward Francisco, "it's your watch now. You got the number to call?"

Francisco nodded and patted his shirt pocket.

"Remember," Big Ed continued, "you see anything that doesn't look right, you call that number."

Francisco nodded again.

Big Ed stood up.

"Francisco."

Francisco looked up at Big Ed.

"You know about Hukai'po, the Night Marchers?"

"Yeah," Francisco said, his throat suddenly dry.

"That's their path," Big Ed said indicating the path he and Francisco had just walked. "But no worries. They only come here now and then. Jus' make sure if you hear 'em, you stay down. Right?"

Francisco could only nod.

"An' don't call about them. Only about things that don't look right to you, okay?"

"Okay," Francisco replied hoarsely.

Big Ed clapped Francisco on the shoulder, slid through the bushes and headed back up the path.

Francisco was alone.

He drank water now and then, stretched as best that he was able and watched the waves roll in and out. He resisted the urge to lay back on the grass since he knew that he might fall asleep. Francisco made a mental note to get a longer nap before coming next time.

Francisco was in the process of yawning and stretching when he heard footsteps. For a moment he was reminded of the Night Marchers, but then a whispered "Watch your step" told him these were the footsteps of living people, not ghosts from ages past.

Francisco watched what he could see of the path through the bushes, and kept still as a mouse.

Three men walked past. Francisco could see that the one leading the way was medium height and overweight. He looked like a haole and carried a flashlight pointed down at the ground. The second man carried a scuba tank, flippers and a mask. The man following him . . . Francisco carefully stood after they passed him. He tried for a better look at this last man. He thought he recognized him. He did. He was called Geoffrey, nicknamed Mento, and Francisco had argued against letting him join the Lua school.

What were these men doing here?

Francisco took out his cellphone and turned it on, holding it under his shirt as he did so in order to keep down the sound of the phone powering on.

He took the paper from his pocket and was about to dial the number on it when he heard some other noise. A noise as of someone, no, many someones, marching along the trail.

Closing his phone Francisco lay down on the ground. Something about the noise of those marching feet raised the hair on the back of his neck.

Francisco covered his head with his arms. His breath came short and labored. He closed his eyes and listened as the sound of feet went marching by him, headed for the beach. Following the same path as the three men who had passed by earlier.

When the marchers had passed Francisco sat up. It was much darker now and try as he could he was unable to see the beach down below.

But he had no trouble hearing. And the screams that he heard coming up from the beach caused him to wet himself. Something he hadn't done since he was a keiki.

GLOSSARY

Wherever possible I have tried, through context, to explain the meaning of some of the Hawaiian words in this story. Just in case I haven't fully succeeded, here are the meanings of those words.

aina	land, earth
aumakua	family guardian
hale	house, building
haole	white person, lit. without breath
hele kaiue	walk with hips swaying
imua	go forward, charge
ka'ane	strangling cord used in lua
kahili	a feathered standard, symbol of royalty
kaiki	young child
kekeface	acne (slang)
lanakila	victory
lei niho palaoa	a carved sperm whale tooth hung on a hair necklace
leiomano	a shark's tooth-studded weapon
lua	Hawaiian martial art
mahu	homosexual either sex (slang, a slur)

malo	a male garment, like a loincloth
momona	fat
ohana	family
'ōlohe lua	lua master
pake	slang for Chinese
pau	finished, quit
pilikia	trouble, bother
poi-dog	mixed-up, blended of many races
wiki wiki	quick, fast

OTHER BOOKS

If you enjoyed this book you should enjoy the others in this series:

The Bones of the Kuhina Nui

The first book of the Kohala Coast Mystery Series. Jealousy and Envy produce Greed. Greed leads to Violence and Violence begets Murder!

An Eric Hoffer Book Award Winner.

The Old Queen's Murder

Second book in the Kohala Coast Mystery Series. A serial killer's arrival on the Big Island brings the Pono family more terror and grief than they have ever known before.

The Old Queen's Treasure

In this third book of the series, Ka iwi, the sacred bones of ancient Hawaiians, intermingle with those of a Chinese treasure ship Captain in this tale of greed and ambition leading to foul murder.

An Eric Hoffer Book Award Finalist

The Old Queen's Guardians

Fourth book of the Kohala Coast Mystery Series. A gang of marijuana growers brings murder to the Old Queen's Beach Resort. Haunani seems to fall further into the fog of Alzheimer's disease. And Teri finds herself having to deal with both problems.

The Old Queen and the Maui Maiden

The fifth book of the series. Teri travels to Maui, directed there by the spirit of Queen Ka'ahumanu, in order to help a long-dead woman. Once there Teri finds her mission threatened by others who want to take the mummified body for themselves in order to profit from it.

The Old Queen and The King

The sixth book of the series. Meet Elvis, a young woman from Kauai, a possible daughter of Elvis and the ghost of Elvis. All mixed together in a murder and the attempt to recover some precious momento.

Or, for a change of pace, try

Primo's: The Kauai Obake Bar

Short stories, humorous and a little spooky, set in a bar in the town of Kapa'a on the island of Kauai. A truly wonderful mix of characters.

Primo's Numbah 2: Is Chicken Skin a Local Delicacy?

More stories about the regulars, and the irregulars, at Primo's Bar on Kauai. Learn what happened when the Air Force dropped an atomic bomb on Kauai — by mistake.

It is burning low,
the tale is on the run.
(Our story is ended.)

www.ingramcontent.com/pod-product-compliance
Lightning Source LLC
Chambersburg PA
CBHW050517260626
47157CB00004B/1358